BCE
GG

D1558829

THE TRAIL TO
MEDICINE LODGE

THE TRAIL TO MEDICINE LODGE

•

TRACY DUNHAM

AVALON BOOKS
THOMAS BOUREGY AND COMPANY, INC.
401 LAFAYETTE STREET
NEW YORK, NEW YORK 10003

PRINTED IN THE UNITED STATES OF AMERICA
ON ACID-FREE PAPER
BY HADDON CRAFTSMEN, SCRANTON, PENNSYLVANIA

THE TRAIL TO
MEDICINE LODGE

Chapter One

Noble McFarland jerked back the dirty tarp and stared at the bodies. The women were lined up, head first, hair matted by powder burns and blood trickling out their ears. Noble didn't look too closely at their faces. A quick glance was enough. The troopers stared in the other direction, as though it would give him privacy. Flies gathered quickly. One of the horses pulling the wagon loaded with the dead women snapped at a horsefly, jangling the traces. There was no other sound. He snapped the canvas back over the figures.

"She's not here. What happened to the escort?" Noble's skin was burned almost to leather by the years he'd spent scouting for the Army, making him look older than his time. Wrinkles creased the edges of his dark blue eyes as he stared at the soldier.

The shavetail lieutenant, nonplussed by the piercing stare, shook his head. "We had to bury them out there. Not enough left to bring back. Looks like they didn't have much time, just enough to kill the women before they got it."

The kid looked green. Noble figured they were close to the same age, but he'd grown up on the frontier.

Long ago he'd seen what Indians could do. To him, it was simply death, it didn't matter how it happened or what was left of your body. He ran a rein-callused hand through his long black hair and found his hat with the other.

"Has anyone told the colonel?" He switched to the trooper who'd ridden in with the news, turning to stare toward headquarters behind his shoulder. They all knew Noble was buying time, trying to avoid the moment when he'd have to face his father.

"Not yet, sir. Figured you'd better do the tellin'."

Noble knew what they all were thinking, that if his sister had been taken alive, he and his father would wish she were dead by now. Trying to clear the lump in his throat, he spit into the dust.

The death wagon hadn't been in the fort more than five minutes. Noble knew his father was already striding out of his office, checking on the commotion, before he saw the troopers snap to attention. Looking every inch the West Pointer he was, the colonel wore his uniform properly buttoned, his brass shining. Even his craggy face, honed by the sun and years of hard riding with his troops, emanated not worry, but control. His father had always commanded instant respect from his men. It was only his son he'd had trouble with.

Colonel Noble McFarland III, U.S.A., saluted the lieutenant. "What's going on, Wheeler?"

Noble had to give the shavetail credit for being cool. He looked at Noble and shook his head slightly.

"Sir, I think your son should do the explaining."

Noble stared at his father, his uniform precise, insignia gleaming like stars in the hot Kansas sun. Noble beat his old hat against the dust on his leather britches, finding it hard to look his father in the eye as he spoke.

"Maybe we'd better discuss this in your office, sir. The escorted wagon got hit, looks like it's the one Beth was supposed to be on."

His father's mouth twitched slightly as he pivoted to stare at the lumps under the tarp. Wheeling on his heel, he threw over his shoulder. "Follow me, scout."

Noble trailed his father into the cool darkness of his office, made out of rough-hewn oaks that had been cut from the banks of the Missouri River. After his eyes adjusted to the dimness of the room, he glimpsed the daguerreotype of Beth clutched in his father's hand. His father stood rooted by his desk, his boots seemingly nailed where he stood. Noble did the same.

"Is she dead?"

Noble had never seen his father so ashen. "Didn't find her body. All the others were shot by the troopers before they got to the men. Escort was pretty mangled. Best if I ride out now, see if I can pick up some tracks."

Noble pivoted. There wasn't anything else to say. His father was a soldier, he'd do what he'd been trained to do, and get his men ready to ride. His father would stop whichever band of Sioux, or Kiowa, or whoever had done this, before they hit some farmer or rancher next. But Noble was just a scout, working on a contract with the Army. He'd have to be the one to try to find Beth, and both of them knew it.

"Take Longwalker. Your sorry excuse for a horse is in no shape to go out again so soon."

Noble stopped in his tracks. He turned to see his father staring at Beth's picture. "Yes sir, I will, and thanks."

Longwalker was the best piece of horseflesh in Kansas. His father understood clearly that Noble had to move fast if Beth was to live. It was almost as good as going himself with Noble. Noble was amazed at the offer. No one had ever ridden the gelding but the colonel. He just hoped the horse would give him the extra bit of luck he was going to need.

It took only a few minutes to pack his gear and stash tins of tomatoes in his saddlebags. Marching into the stables, Noble headed straight for Longwalker's stall. The big bay wickered a soft greeting.

"Sorry, friend, no sugar today," Noble apologized. "We've got hard work out there waitin' for us."

The men of the post stared as he led Longwalker from his stall and mounted up. If it hadn't been such a tragedy, Noble would have been tempted to grin at them from Longwalker's sixteen-hand height. As it was, he focused on the directions given him by the lieutenant, directions that would take him back to where it had started, the massacre that was changing their lives faster than an Army transfer.

The sky was too clear and blue, the clouds too puffy

and picturesque. Noble had lived all his life in Indian territories, and had learned the hard way that something bad had to follow such clear and perfect weather. If it had been any other time, Noble would have reveled in Longwalker's smooth canter, the easy, surefooted way the big horse traversed the miles without breaking a sweat. But it wasn't another day, and while he knew it was useless, he wanted to whip the half-thoroughbred into a dead run. But he knew better. They'd both need some energy later on, after he found the tracks.

He pushed Longwalker toward the bluffs where the bodies had been found, his instincts alert to every blade of buffalo grass and shadow for some sign of the path the renegades had taken with Beth. He couldn't afford the time it would take to stop and study the landscape before striking on. The stench of burned hair and flesh told him he'd found where it had happened, before he saw the charred wagon rims splintered in their iron hoops. The hot summer wind carried the odor as a warning that the Indians weren't as tame as the settlers had been lulled into believing. The troopers who'd found the site had left it as it was, except for four shallow graves hurriedly hacked out for the men they'd pieced together. Trunks and bonnets lay in grotesque positions, strewn about the death site like flowers scattered from the graves.

Noble dismounted, hanging Longwalker's reins. The horse began to graze, unconcerned with the carnage that had happened here. Noble scooped from under the toppled wagon a small, black taffeta bonnet, twirling it abstractly as he surveyed the scene. The troopers had trampled any identifying tracks he might have found. He'd have to start circling in wider loops.

Throwing his boot in the stirrup, his eye was caught by one of the opened trunks. The Indians had looted what they wished, but this one seemed too full. He led Longwalker over to the pressed leather trunk, fear knotting his gut. He knew why the Indians hadn't wanted anything in this one.

It was filled with books. Opening one of the red leather volumes, he stared at the thin, delicate handwriting on the flyleaf: "Property of Elizabeth McFarland."

He snapped it shut, placing it carefully in his saddlebag. Now he knew for sure that if she was out there, she'd be alive. He knew Beth. She was probably the only one of the women on the wagon who would have been carrying her own weapon. She knew how to use it. Maybe that was why they'd captured her, and not left her raped flesh to rot. Noble knew the Indians admired courage. Beth had plenty of that.

He'd just come in from a long reconnaissance and hadn't seen any signs of trouble. They'd truly believed the Kiowa were under control. The attack on the wagonload of women coming back from a shopping expedition to Kansas City had been totally unexpected. His father would never have permitted the trip if they'd had the slightest suspicion trouble was brewing. Beth had just finished her degree at a fancy ladies' seminary in New England, a course of action his father had insisted on, and was coming home to the life they'd both lived as long as they could remember. Their mother had been one of those Army wives who had insisted on accompanying her husband everywhere he was sent, and even after she'd died of cholera, their father had kept the children with him. Politely, he'd turned down offers from well-meaning relatives back East to provide a "real" home for the motherless Noble and Beth. They were a family.

Beth had been the one who was good with book learning. While she studied the Greek and Latin assignments their father wrote out daily, Noble would sneak off to play with his Indian friends, children of the post tribes that had been emasculated and domesticated by alcohol and Army rations while the buffalo became scarce. Noble had learned the local dialects, how the Indians thought, and most of all, how they killed. The Army scouts, mostly local Indians who had started young working for the Army, had taken Noble under their wing, and taught him the tracking language that made the Army so dependent on them to find the enemy.

Noble stroked Longwalker's shiny neck and imagined what he would do after the attack on the wagon, if he'd been a brave. He'd keep up the attack, count coup, steal as much stock as he could. The ladies' trunks of clothes and books weren't enough to eat or

to raise their prestige when they got back to the main
tribe. The troopers had been few. Noble touched his
heels to Longwalker, moving out at a slow trot. He
didn't have any time to waste. Longwalker's silky canter ate up the miles. Then he saw it.

The buzzards formed a black clump in the grass.
Noble spurred the bay to a gallop, sliding his carbine
from its holster, just in case. The birds barely ruffled
their wings as he charged into their midst.

Noble cringed at the reason why the buzzards were
so reluctant to fly at the sight of him. They'd found a
feast to last them several days. He dismounted, firing
at a few of the carrion birds. They toppled over, sending the others into a screeching retreat.

The figure on the ground was once an Indian. Noble
checked what was left of his paint and the beadwork,
and knew he was right about the Kiowa. A slight wind
ruffled the Indian's long hair, and Noble could see
through the bird's wounds that the man had been shot.
Jerking out his bone-handled knife, he dug into the
Indian's back. The bullet was still there, much flat-
tened. Wiping it on the grass, Noble fingered its ridges.
It had come from an old-fashioned cavalry horse pistol,
just like the kind their father had given Beth when he'd
taught her to shoot.

Noble pocketed the bullet. The Indians would use
Beth until they tired of her. But at least one of them
wasn't getting any warrior's funeral. They would de-
spise a brother who had been killed by a woman. Or

the act would have given Beth some prestige, some special medicine. They might honor her bravery, and perhaps let her live. If not, her power would at least give her the right to a quicker death.

Noble mounted. At least Beth had had some small measure of revenge, and she was still alive.

Noble pushed Longwalker until the light faded at long last. He didn't want to put the gelding in a gopher hole. Hunkering down to a cold dinner, Noble tallied the options. His bet was on another raid, then back to the main tribe to show their spoils and have a party. If Beth were going to make it, she'd have to still be alive when they headed for home. That would mean they were keeping her for a slave, or to sell to some other tribe. If she hadn't made it that far, she was dead already.

Noble dreaded the thought of having to tell the colonel he'd found her body. He pushed the image from his mind as he rolled up in his saddle blanket. It was going to be hard to sleep, knowing Beth was out there waiting for him to find her.

They'd been close as children. Each had known what the other would say before the words could come tumbling out. Beth always stuck up for him when the wrath of their father would threaten to drive him off to live with his Indian friends. Intervening, she could explain their father's viewpoint to Noble so clearly that Noble felt he had to forgive his father for not understanding him.

It had become devastatingly clear that Noble would never become the West Pointer his father had planned. Noble instead had started riding out with the scouts when he was still just a boy. Finally, his father had given up and let him go his own way.

Only Beth had done what was expected of her. Their father had sent her away as soon as she'd shown signs of budding into a beauty. Her golden hair was a deeper echo of their mother's, but Beth had their father's piercing blue eyes. Tall and willow-waisted, she carried herself naturally with an inborn grace that was unusual in girls that age. Now, because she'd gone away to school, she was either dead or as good as. For a second, Noble blamed their father for sending her to Massachusetts, and in the next instance realized he was being unfair. Beth wouldn't have wanted him to blame the colonel. She had an incredible ability to remain fair, even when they fought as children.

His head on his saddle for a pillow, Noble remembered the horror stories they told each other about Indians capturing and torturing whites, each trying to outscare the other as they hid under the blue Dresden plate quilt their mother had made when they were small. He tried to shut out the pictures of what was happening to Beth now. Even if he found her alive, he feared she'd never again be the same Beth he'd loved. For sure, she'd never again be accepted by the other white women on the post.

The first morning light released him from his nightmare. Slurping his canteen, he pulled a piece of jerky from his saddlebags for a quick breakfast. Saddling Longwalker, he was pleased the horse was still frisky after their long day before. Today he should find fresh tracks, if he was moving as fast as he thought he was in the correct direction.

Checking the horizon, he sensed it was going to be another scorcher. The land was bone dry, only wild prairie grass keeping it from becoming an ocean of dust. It was getting to be time for a twister, he decided. There was something definitely wrong with the blue of the sky.

He'd found the tracks by noon. They were through killing for the joy of it, now they wanted cattle. It was easier to pick off herds than to wait for maggoty beef from the government. He felt the damp ground at the edge of a barely trickling creek. One of the hoof impressions was deeper than the others. Could mean a heavier horse, or two riders on one back. The second option was the only one he chose to accept. That would mean he'd found the right tracks, and was that much closer to Beth.

Chapter Two

Beth gritted her teeth, clutching the skin of the Indian who'd thrown her over the sharp withers of the blanketless pony. She'd be shamed if she screamed at the agony of the pinto's bone cutting into her thighs, so she dug her nails into the leg of the Kiowa who'd taken her Colt and tied her on the pony like a sack of potatoes.

She'd killed one. It had taken awhile for his lungs to fill up with his own blood, but her bullet had done it. They'd left him behind, no warrior's burial for him. The Kiowa who held her pinned to the back of his horse had snatched her pistol, knocking her sideways with a blow from his fist. But he hadn't killed her. Instead, he'd lashed her like a hog for butchery while they had their way with the other women on the transport. The troopers still barely alive had been staked and eviscerated. Their screams still shrilled through her brain.

Even though she'd shut her eyes and prayed for a quick death for them all, it hadn't been quick enough. And still they'd left her alone. She didn't know why, except perhaps they were saving her for a special treat for later.

The Kiowa stopped only a few hours at night, obviously knowing exactly where they were going. There was nothing aimless about their journey. Beth wished once more she'd kept a knife in her boot, as she'd done when she was a child. At first, she'd been copying her older brother, but later, she'd learned to use it so well she could protect herself if she had to. She cursed herself for becoming so darned much an Easterner that she'd forgotten the basic lessons of survival on the frontier. Thinking of how she'd escape kept her mind from picturing what they planned for her body. The leather wrapped on her wrists and ankles cut deeper into her flesh as she struggled against the constraints.

She figured that by now the troops had found what was left of the transport wagon and its escort. They'd probably written her off for dead, or as good as, unless Noble had been around in time to do something about it. The chances of Noble being at the fort when the news got back about the transport were slim, she knew. He spent as little time as he could near their father.

She realized that she was going to have to depend on herself to stay alive. Right now, that meant she'd do whatever she had to do. Because the longer she was alive, the better her chances of staying alive.

She jounced with the pace of the pony, his hooves clipping much too swiftly. She still didn't have a plan, but all that mattered in that instant was the pain in her abdomen. Suddenly, one of the Kiowa reined in, and the Indian whose thigh she'd clutched shoved her down from the horse.

Her skirt over her shoulders, she sprawled in the grass. This was what she'd been expecting, that they'd finally have their fun with her. She searched their faces for lust, but they stared away from her, toward the horizon. The Indian who'd carried her so far leaned over, jerking her toward him by her hair. Swiftly he wrapped a leather thong around her mouth so tightly she couldn't move her tongue. Throwing her sideways, he looped the end of the thong around her wrists and then her ankles. Her stomach heaved with fear.

She could see, finally, what they'd spied long before her eyes had adjusted to the distance. A small, thin loop of smoke rose from a sod shanty on the horizon. A few cattle, barely a dozen, swished their tails as they grazed. She wanted to scream a warning as the Kiowa raced away from her toward the soddy.

They were at a dead run, hanging low, their bows and ancient rifles ready to shoot. Suddenly, the cattle spooked, bellowing as they stampeded. Racing from the shack at the sound, the two white men were killed almost instantly. It seemed to take only minutes, then the Kiowa rounded up the cattle and trotted back in her direction. She searched desperately for a depression where she could hide from their hooves, but knew in an instant she was tied too tightly to squirm. *Dear Lord,* she prayed, *this might be a better way to die, but I'd at least like a fighting chance.* She remembered the trooper's startled face when she'd pulled the cavalry pistol from her carpetbag and had begun firing at the Kiowa when they attacked the transport. She would have killed the private if he'd aimed his pistol at her, but the Indians had gotten him first.

The pinto pony that had been the source of her torture suddenly swooped down on her. The brave riding him leaned over and scooped her under her arm as though she were a pitcher of water. With the other hand he sliced the thong and dumped her once more before him over the withers. At least this time she landed astride the animal, she thought gratefully as she grabbed a handful of mane. She tried to clamp her knees onto the horse's thin shoulders, but her petticoats were in the way.

Jerking between the iron arms of the brave like a puppet, she gritted her teeth to bear the pain once more. The pony never broke stride as the Indians drove the cattle, now lowing with fatigue. Her throat screamed for water, while her muscles cramped so severely she began to lose consciousness after several hours of the hard ride. Her mind left the present, and she saw herself as a child.

Just as she began to feel safe within her childhood memories, she realized that the swirl of dust she'd been breathing thickened. Sputtering, she gagged for breath. The Kiowa reined in. Opening her eyes, Beth suddenly realized they'd reached a small camp.

Now she had to make her move. It had come to her, in her memories of her childhood, that the Indians thought anyone who was crazy, or God-touched as they called it, was not to be harmed. She'd pretend to be someone else, someone not in her right mind.

The brave flopped her off the pinto, wrenching up her head by her hair. The squaws and children gathered around them, yelling and shouting, some waving the cattle into a crude remuda. The braves showed off their trophies.

Beth struggled with nausea when she saw Mrs. Breaker's rich russet tresses on a lance. One of the braves reached over to fondle Beth's blond hair. The Indian who'd carted her around on his pinto pushed the other's hand off her.

"I'm sure you would all like to hear the *Iliad* and the *Odyssey,* declaimed in the original Greek." She smiled, using her best finishing-school voice. "But first, I must be properly attired for my performance."

Grinning again, she stared into the eyes of the squaws and braves surrounding her. A few shifted uneasily, as though captives never spoke.

Wrenching off her blouse, Beth unbuttoned her petticoat. Wearing her corset, shift, stockings, and boots, she hummed loudly a hymn. Running her fingers through her hair, she plastered a big smile on her face, and began to recite the *Iliad.* Using her hands to gesticulate at the high points, she pretended she was back at the academy, performing to a theater full of appreciative students. Every now and then, she'd drop a dazzling smile, touched with an edge of craziness, into her repertoire. Her voice became shrill as she told in ancient Greek of the Trojan Wars.

The Kiowa muttered, shifting uneasily. Finally, a few backed away as Beth raised her voice as though they were deaf. A small child prodded her bravely with a stick, and she pretended it was unfelt. He poked her again, and she pivoted, folding her arms around him, reciting even more loudly. The other children ran.

The women were the first to back away, making signs she guessed were necessary to ward off evil spirits. She batted her lashes at them, grinning lopsidedly. Her plan was working. Slowly the men gathered by the women, ignoring her. She sensed disgust on the face of the brave who'd claimed her for his own.

She was rooted where she'd been dropped from the pinto, reciting every line she could dredge up, making up others, gesticulating wildly, her voice hysterical. By nightfall, she knelt in the same spot, her voice barely a whisper after hours of recitation. Every Indian passing her way gave her wide berth. She started with modern poetry next. She had to use a chamber pot in the worst way. She wet her bloomers, and didn't care. She was still alive.

Chapter Three

Noble scented the bodies of the two men by the shanty. They'd just relaxed after rigor mortis, so he figured he wasn't more than a day off the trail of the right band of Kiowa. They'd move more slowly, herding cattle, taking time to slaughter some first and have a big feast.

Suddenly, he hauled on Longwalker's reins. In a matted patch of prairie grass, he caught a glint of metal. Dismounting, he scooped up the ear bob, broken from its hook. He snapped a fist over the filigreed gold, and tried to force air in his lungs. It was an earring he'd seen often on his mother's portrait on his father's big Army desk. Beth had worn them when she became sixteen. Beth was still with the Kiowa, and still alive.

Throwing his leg over the saddle, he roweled Longwalker. The gelding sashayed and snorted. Be calm, Noble told himself, as Longwalker stretched into a canter, you can't afford a broken leg on this horse. He hauled the bay's bit, slowing Longwalker to an easy trot. He'd ride until the sun was low on the horizon.

Pitching camp with the last of the light, he settled down for another cold camp. He'd watered the horse at the raided ranch, where, thankfully, the well hadn't been polluted. But he couldn't push the gelding as hard as the Kiowa pushed their ponies. Longwalker wasn't accustomed to hard usage, and he'd be no good to Noble lame.

Noble swallowed some dry rations and shoved his brim down over his eyes. He was just beginning to drift into a worried half-sleep when his instincts told him something was wrong, very wrong. Longwalker snorted lightly, swishing his tail as he pranced slightly.

Reaching for his rifle, Noble snapped it up to fire when a slight figure leaped on his back, wrenching the weapon from his fists. Noble could smell Indian, and twisted for his knife.

"Hey, stupid, it's me, I've tracked you for the past two days."

Noble gasped for air, relaxing. "You scared the stuffin' out of me, Johnny! What you doing out here? Thought you were with Gordon, further west?" Noble reached for his flint to start a small fire, so he could see his childhood friend, Johnny Two Hats. In the shadows, Johnny looked all Indian, except for his Army hat and shirt. Noble knew his father had been a white soldier. But Johnny still wore the soft leather leggings and some of the beadwork of his mother's tribe, the Comanche. Johnny was more Indian than white; Noble had seen the half-Comanche smell Indians before anyone else among the scouts.

"Got back just after you lit out. Gordon sent me to

warn the colonel about the Kiowa. Day late, dollar short, huh, pal?'' Johnny cocked his hat. ''Colonel sent me after you, help find Beth. Guess you haven't seen her body yet?''

Noble pulled the ear bob from his pocket. ''Found this back at the ranch. She's still with them.''

Johnny jerked off his Army cap and shook down his long, Indian-length hair. He jammed it under the hat when with most white men, but he and Noble had been friends since boyhood. ''Moving fast, friend. But you're thinking too hard about Beth. You'd have picked me up long ago if you'd been awake. You're a better scout than that, amigo.''

Noble shook his head ruefully. ''Right, Johnny. I keep fearing I'll find her, then again, it might be better if she were dead. This bunch is riding hard and fast, and they know exactly what they want. Beth was probably just extra booty, something to trade. They'll hide with the beef for a while, then go get some more when that's eaten.''

''Yeah, I'd say you're right. Times are tough right now, it's a pretty hungry crowd. Too few buffalo to keep hungry stomachs from pitchin' a fit, rotten government rations, and winter not so far away. Signs all say it'll be a hard one.''

''I just hope it's only food they want, not women. Beth is tough, but I don't know how much even she can take.''

Johnny stared into the night, avoiding the look in

his friend's eyes. The agony was too personal. "Remember when she shot that rattler going after her dog? Skinned it to make herself a hat band. How old was she then, maybe eleven?"

"Yeah, that was something. But she's been back East for two years now. No telling what sort of foolishness they drilled into her. She's probably such a lady, she's forgotten everything we ever taught her. If she can just not panic. . . . "

Johnny pulled his saddle blanket from his horse, stretching it before the low fire. "She's alive so far, she hasn't panicked yet. But don't get your hopes too high." He didn't want Noble to know the colonel had sent him specifically to keep Noble from getting himself killed, that he believed Beth was dead already.

Johnny settled down. "Sleep, pal. We got some hard riding ahead of us."

Noble kicked the fire to ashes. "You'd better keep up, Johnny. I won't be waiting for all your fancy circling around. I know where they're heading." There was an edge sharp with fear in Noble's voice that Johnny hadn't heard before.

Johnny was worried. He'd never seen Noble lose his nerve. He didn't want him doing it for the first time in the middle of a band of renegade Kiowa.

They didn't bother with breakfast. Noble and Johnny saddled up before dawn, edging their way in the early gray light. They didn't need words to urge each other on. Expectancy hung about them like capes. Noble hadn't decided what they'd do when they found the renegades, but he did know he wasn't the one who was going to hightail it back to the fort for reinforcements.

The trail was clear, the cattle were being pushed hard. Noble thought it unusual the band hadn't stopped for a quick meal of beef. It could mean several things, one of which was that this band wasn't starving yet. It could also mean they were planning on rejoining their main tribe before celebrating. Noble didn't relish the thought of Beth in the hands of even more of them.

"Any ideas?" It was Johnny who finally broke the silence as the morning light rouged the sky. It was going to be a scorcher.

" 'Bout what?" Noble kept his eyes on the horizon.

"Don't play games with me, my friend. I always beat you. They're meeting up with the rest of their tribe. No way we can take 'em on. Got anything to trade with? Not that this group's in a trading mood, but we can try. . . . "

Noble snorted. "No chance. They'll keep her, get more for her south of the border. Or use her. All we got that they want is sitting here on our hips, and I'm not about to trade guns for Beth. She'd have my hide."

"We'd never make it without those guns." Johnny was firm.

Noble fidgeted with his reins. "We can try to trade 'em Longwalker. Not another piece of horseflesh around can match him."

"They'll want more, and you know it."

Noble groaned. Maybe one of them should head for the fort. But as soon as the Kiowa got wind of moving troops, Beth was dead. He'd have to be in the camp when that happened.

"So who's riding back?" Noble already had his hand in his pocket to fish out a coin to flip.

"You are, pal."

Noble shook his shaggy head at his friend, grinning. "That's not gonna happen, and you know it."

"You're on the fastest horse. I can speak Kiowa, yours is nonexistent. I'm Indian. You're not. Have I pointed out enough of the obvious?"

Noble searched his friend's hard eyes, sensing they'd come to a division they could never rejoin. "You take Longwalker back. I'm staying on the trail."

A rumble from the horizon shook the horses to a skitter, sending each man grabbing the reins more tightly.

"What the . . . " Noble pulled an old-fashioned spyglass from his saddle roll. But he didn't need it to see what was coming.

"Any shelter you can see?" Johnny pivoted in his saddle. "It'll hit in less than an hour."

Already the sky purpled, rolling black clouds along like dust balls.

"Got a slicker?" Noble hopped down, flicking his pack loose. "We'll have to hobble the horses and try to keep the rifles dry. . . . "

"Not gonna happen, and you know it. Main thing

we gotta do is keep out of its way. Can you see which way it's headin'?'' Johnny sat rock-solid in his saddle.

"Why, you gonna outrun a twister?" Noble snorted. "Can't do it. Let's batten down."

"Nope, I'm not sticking around. Maybe we've got time."

Noble hesitated. There was another slash of lightning on the horizon. "All right. Wind's coming up due west. We hightail it east." But that would take them away from Beth, he realized. And any rain will wipe out the tracks. But he knew Johnny was right. There was no right choice, either way—running or staying, it was a risk.

The heat radiating in the early morning sun wafted suddenly with the scent of cordite. The cumulonimbus clouds were stacked up on the horizon like firewood about to ignite, darkening with each flash of lightning. Noble threw his slicker over his shoulders, tossing his bedroll cover to Johnny. Their greased and seasoned holsters for the rifles and guns would have to keep them dry, he thought as Longwalker's neck slicked with sweat. The horse sensed the danger in the sky.

Johnny pushed to a gallop. Longwalker stretched it further, as the hot, wet smell of long-dry earth, suddenly soaked, muscled into the smell of cordite. Noble hunkered down, wondering how long they could keep up this pace. It was a futile gesture, trying to outrun a storm of this magnitude. But if Johnny wanted to try, he'd go along with him.

The gust hit them in the back just as Noble shouted. He tried again as Johnny shook his head and cupped an ear.

"Whoever makes it out of this, keeps on looking. Until she's found. Right?"

This time Johnny heard him. Nodding his assent, he held Noble's eyes with a promise both knew would never be broken. The next instant, the storm struck them with the force of a steam engine.

Noble was torn from Longwalker, hurtling to the ground as though he were a twig wrested from a branch. Even as the icy rain pounded into him, he clutched Longwalker's reins, digging his nails into the rain-slick leather. Longwalker screamed. Rolling facedown in the grass, Noble dug every inch of his body into the ground, feeling grass and grit in his teeth as the icy wind and rain slashed into him.

Longwalker shrilled again, whipping his head free from Noble's clutches. "Johnny?" Noble struggled to lift his head to find his friend, clutched for rain-slick reins, and lost them. The driving rain bit into his face as he saw a blur beside him, hooves flying, and a salvo of dirt. He could only pray Johnny was alive.

Shrieking like a demon, the wind and funnel tore around them, hurling debris and death. The icy rain stung Noble's skin, and he knew his clothing had been shredded from his back. He'd never felt such fear. There was no way out, no way to escape or fight back against this devil of nature. Silently he prayed for them all, man and horse.

Suddenly, it was gone. His ears ringing, Noble unclutched the earth, wiping mud from his eyes as he dared lift his head. A hardy, steady rain plunged into his face, but it was nothing like the icy needles that had stung him like a porcupine. A tangle of horses sprawled about fifty feet from him. He couldn't see Johnny.

On hands and knees, he rocked himself free from his haven. Finally able to stand, he leaned into the downpour, shading his eyes with both palms.

''Johnny,'' he shouted. His voice sounded like mice chattering. Pivoting, he tried again. A small, dark heap he'd thought was a boulder started untwisting. Racing to Johnny, Noble felt his heart in his throat as he saw, at last, blood running freely from Johnny's bare back.

''We made it,'' Noble tried to give himself false hope as he spoke into Johnny's ear. Johnny had stopped moving.

Reaching under the mat of wet hair, Noble found Johnny's pulse at the side of his neck. He still breathed! If only there was a way to get him dry and covered, Noble thought worriedly as he probed gently with his fingers. Somehow he had to get into some shelter, and see how much damage there was.

Johnny groaned, trying to roll over.

''Stay put, old friend. I'm gonna check the horses.'' Johnny moaned in response.

Trudging through the ever-lessening rain to the heap he knew was horseflesh, Noble felt a sharp stab in his ribs he'd managed to ignore until then. With each step the hot needles took another jab, and he knew he'd cracked a few ribs in the fall from Longwalker. *God,* he prayed, *if that's the worst of it, I'll be eternally grateful.* Wiping the blood from his eyes, he roughly swiped a nick in his forehead.

Shutting his eyes as he stumbled up to the horses, he knew he didn't want to open them. There was no reason for him to look, he didn't have a dry chamber in the pistol on his hip to finish off the poor beasts.

There was no need. Longwalker's neck was broken, Johnny's pinto had snapped his back. Dirt and debris matted their still-warm hides. Longwalker's right leg protruded into the pinto's belly. It had probably happened as they slammed into each other, Noble realized as he mourned for the horses. His father would understand, but forgiveness was another matter. Longwalker had been his pride and joy, right after Beth.

They'd have to walk back to the fort and hope the colonel had sent someone out after them as reinforcements. Unless he could come up with some help, it was the end of the search for Beth. His insides were as icy cold as his hands.

"Johnny," he tried again as the scout lay motionless. "You've got to try, Johnny. We've gotta get going, no way out but hoofin' it. I know, it's against

your principles to walk, but the horses are dead.''
Noble didn't know if Johnny could hear him.

At least his own voice kept him from sinking down beside Johnny and burying his face in the mud. He couldn't give up, and neither could Johnny. Ignoring the agony in his side, Noble edged his friend onto his back, arching over him to keep as much of the lessening wet off him as he could. Johnny's face was gray.

It was bad. But Noble had seen worse. Johnny would make it. He had to. Noble needed him to find Beth. Suddenly, Noble remembered the times as children when Beth and Johnny had gone off together, the two of them conspiring against Noble. Even as children they'd had a special bond. There was a reason Johnny had shown up at the post when he did, and hightailed it after Noble. Noble refused to believe that fate would give him his friend on the most important track of his life, and then take him away.

Johnny's eyelids fluttered, then slit open. Noble smiled. They'd make it, somehow. Then they'd find Beth. That was what he'd tell his father, once they got back to the post.

It was a long, bitterly hungry walk back. The open plains had been changed by the twister into a landscape they couldn't recognize. For three agonizing days, the two men took it inch by inch, using all their will and self-encouragement to reach the post.

Teetering on the outskirts, Johnny and Noble clung to each other. Finally, as though someone took the time to use a glass to check out the two men on foot, a shout echoed from the post.

"Thank goodness, we made it." Noble grinned wolfishly at his friend. "Wanna bet how long it takes my father to ask when we're riding out again?"

"No bets, friend. You always win." The gash over Johnny's eye was a ragged brown line. "Tape those ribs up, you'll be whipping on out ahead of me, that's for sure."

They laughed as though drunk, too silly for more words, ecstatic they'd survived. The sounds died in their throats as they saw who rode out to greet them.

"My father, wouldn't you know," Noble muttered.

Johnny waved a slight salute. It wouldn't take Noble long to get them provisioned to get out of there, fast.

Chapter Four

Beth awoke to a toe in her rump. A haggard old woman squatted near her, a gourd bowl in hand. Beth grinned her maniacal smile and reached for the food. The woman shoved it toward her, mumbling under her breath as she shuffled off.

Beth shoved the thick mush in her mouth as fast as she could. She almost gagged, her swollen throat was too tender to swallow. But she forced another mouthful. Her fair skin was burned scarlet from the beating it had taken from the sun, and her eyes felt swollen and hot. She rubbed a fingerful of the mush on her eyelids, hoping it would help the sting.

There was a modicum of relief. Grateful, Beth wiped some more mush across her cheeks and forehead. When she opened her eyes, a gaggle of children were pointing and laughing. Beth smiled again.

Spreading a thin layer of the gruel on her shoulders and bare neck, she gestured for the children to come so she could paint them too. They ran from her hands screaming.

Finally the old woman reappeared, snatching the bowl from Beth. Then she turned, motioning for Beth

to follow her. Beth glanced hurriedly around the camp.
They seemed to be taking down the tepees and loading
the travois. No one paid any attention to her.

It was easier to follow the old woman than to stay
where she was. Reciting the 93rd Psalm, she stumbled
on numbed feet after the hag. The crone was wrinkled
like cracked mud, her skin parched and dark walnut.
Two greasy gray braids hung over the woman's
stooped, thin shoulders.

Reaching a tattered tepee, the woman tossed a ragged
piece of skin at Beth. Realizing it had a hole in the
middle, Beth surmised the woman intended her to wear
it. Gratefully she poked her head through. It hung
loosely, but would keep the sun off her shoulders.

The travois were being loaded quickly around them.
The old woman shoved Beth to the tepee, gesturing
she was to help her in its dismantling. Beth stood, her
hands at her sides. If she helped the old woman, she
lost her status as a crazy one. If she didn't help her,
she'd probably die of hunger or thirst, before too long.

She made her choice. Untying the leather thongs,
she tried to seem oblivious to the hubbub around her.
It was a trick, she decided, the ability to sink into
another world in her mind. She made herself remember
her cool, snowbound school in Massachusetts even as
she balanced the tepee poles over her burned shoulder.

The old woman strung a hide across two poles and
tied them to Beth's back. So she was to be a beast of
burden. She waited calmly as the hag stacked her par-

fleches and meager belongings on the travois she'd fashioned behind Beth. Finally, as it seemed everyone else had strung out on the path ahead, the crone poked Beth in the ribs, muttering and gesturing for Beth to follow.

Beth's black high-button shoes had rubbed her feet raw by noon. But she trudged on, feeling the lodge poles cutting into her shoulders. If she were a slave, so be it. It surprised her still that the brave who'd taken such pains to haul her back to his camp hadn't claimed her. Somehow, her feigned insanity and the protection of the old woman had given her the invisibility she'd wanted. She wouldn't complain.

The crone tossed her a few handfuls from a basket that night, after Beth struggled with the lodge poles, to the best of her understanding of the hag's muttered directions. The old woman had shaken her head at Beth's clumsiness, snatching poles and thongs from her as Beth quaked in bewilderment and fear. The tattered robes wrapped the poles under the adroit hands of the woman, as Beth tried to help. The hag's strength amazed Beth.

The band moved fast, the braves herding the cows and horses as though they were on the run. Beth guessed at the miles, surprised every day at the distance they seemed to have come. This band was small, with few women and children. It was part of a larger band, she guessed, these few having gone raiding in the last days of summer. The old woman continued to screech at Beth, driving her with a stick like a donkey. Beth curled each night by the edge of the tatterdemalion tepee, grateful for each mouthful the woman shoved at her, for her life, for every thing large and small that she could think of. She was kept alive by a strange mélange of gratitude and hatred for these people who held her captive.

They were moving too fast. Counting the days since her capture, she knew she should have seen signs of the Army by now. But the feeling in the camp was one of driving to a destination, not away from anything they feared. The old woman drove herself and Beth mercilessly. Beth wondered why she'd come along on a hunting raid. The majority of braves and the scarcity of children and squaws meant only those who could travel quickly had been chosen to go.

Her boots lost their heels, and she chewed a hole for her toes through the leather. Barefoot, she'd never make it. Any hint of fat dropped from her, until she could feel her bones like spoons arranged in a drawer. Feeling herself toughen physically as the miles rolled under her feet, she once again planned her escape. This time it would be easier to accomplish.

She hadn't yet figured out why the poor, haggard old woman was with this marauding band. Her inability to answer that one question gnawed at Beth. Somehow, she knew the answer was important.

Chapter Five

Johnny and Noble stared at each other, dirt, fatigue, and anxiety cutting lines into their young faces.

"It's cold. Gone." Johnny Two Hats settled on his rump and shook his head. "Not a danged thing we coulda done better, that's the hard part."

Noble rocked back in the saddle, pulling a trailworn map from his saddlebags. It had taken longer than either expected to heal from the effects of the twister. Johnny's broken arm had festered during the long days it took them to trudge back to the post, and for a while, it had looked like gangrene. Noble's ribs had healed quickly, but for days he'd seen two or three of everything and a quick breath still stabbed him. Both of them had seethed with anger at the physical limitations that kept them from hitting the trail again.

"Looks to me like we gotta take an educated guess, this point on."

Johnny glanced disdainfully at the map. "Not gonna do you any good, them chicken-scratchings."

Temper flaring, Noble jerked to face his friend. "Got any better ideas?"

Grinning like a lizard on a hot rock, Johnny slithered

up in his saddle. "You know me, *compadre,* always got an ace up my sleeve."

Noble knew he was bluffing, trying to humor him. "Yeah, sure." The end of summer was slipping away from them like the miles they'd covered searching for Beth.

"Might as well make camp." Noble uncinched the saddle, rubbing his horse's back with a handful of rough grass. "Not much light left."

The colonel hadn't said much when Noble had told him about Longwalker. Noble had taken care to explain that the horse hadn't suffered; the broken neck must have been instantaneous. It was then that Noble had realized how completely his father was wrapped up in finding Beth. Normally, he'd have ranted at the heavens, at the very least, cursing the death of the thoroughbred. But the gray-haired man had just suddenly looked older when Noble managed to blurt out the news.

The colonel had asked next, addressing the question over his shoulder as if afraid to face his son, if it would do any good to send out another search party. They both had known the trail was washed away, that it would be a matter now of painstakingly combing every inch of the territory for signs, of asking questions of the right people. The men his father had sent out had returned in their allotted three weeks with nothing but footsore horses.

"Umph." Landing on his toes, Johnny slid his small

Indian saddle from his horse. "What you say I go home?"

"Back to the fort? Getting too much for you, Johnny?" Noble threw the coffee beans into the battered pot, jamming it in the small fire he'd nursed into existence. Anxiety was making him testy, and he knew it.

Johnny stared at his friend through hooded eyes. Suddenly, slipping his knife from his beaded belt, he tossed it at Noble's foot.

"Mind you of anything?"

Smoothing the finely honed blade on his leg, Noble stroked the knife. "Yeah, guess so. Still got the scar, suppose I always will." Noble flashed his palm, a thin white line crossing it diagonally. They'd mingled their blood when just children.

"Me too." Johnny matched his friend's palm to his. "Not the fort, you donkey, home to my tribe. Best way I know to hear what's going on, any white women show up in the slave trade."

Noble paled slightly. "Long shot. You may hear nothing for months. Won't put your stock up with the Army, either." But this time some of the deadness had left his voice. "May not be safe, think of that? Just may have figgered out you went white a long ways back, only reason for heading for home is to lead the Army down their trail."

"I'll take my chances. Beth's running outta hers right fast."

Noble stared at his friend, blue eyes meeting black. "God, I hope not."

"It's been too long. Winter's early. We don't do something now, we'll have to wait for Spring for sure."

Noble shut his eyes, seeing Beth frozen in the drifts of winter. He knew Johnny was right, they had to split up.

"How will we let each other know?" The panic in his thought ran down to his toes.

"Not much I'll be able to do. You send your news back to the fort, I'll try to check up whenever I can. You find her first, don't worry about me. I'll get back when I can. If I find her, you'll know. Your father will find a way to get the word out."

Noble settled back, letting his feet warm by the small fire. It was getting colder at night, there was no doubt about it. The tornado had destroyed anything that would have given them a way to find Beth. Still, a small voice in the back of his mind said it was a bad idea to split up, that they needed each other's different strengths and skills working together to find her.

"OK. I'll go along with you for now. Those Comanche take your scalp, I'll sure miss you." It was the closest Noble could come to admitting his worry.

"Hang onto your own head of hair, pal." Johnny snorted softly. They both knew the odds were against them. But they'd do whatever it took. Beth's life depended upon it. If she were still alive . . .

Chapter Six

Johnny hunkered down on the bluff, watching the slender figures below him scurry about in the Indian encampment. He and Noble had set their rendezvous three months from now, and he hadn't a moment to waste. The last raids of the autumn were going to be in full swing, and he had to prove he was one of them again. His hair was pulled back and tied with an eagle feather, his paint was carefully drawn in vermilion to show his battle coups, and a red hand on his chest denoted hand-to-hand combat with an enemy. He felt ready. Although he would never have told Noble, each instant he was free of the white man's clothes and customs was heaven to him.

Carefully spreading out his treasures, Johnny fingered the pipe, three perfectly round black stones he'd found as a boy, his rifle, the woven blanket that had been Noble's gift to him many years ago, and the small medicine pouch containing the shriveled remnants of his umbilical cord and other magic items his mother had collected from his birth. His mother's quill work on the pouch still held the best magic Johnny had ever known.

Fingering the pouch gently, he remembered how he'd tried to get Beth to make a similar pouch for Noble when they were children. She'd turned up with bit of yellow silk embroidered with a bunch of sadly knotted pink roses. The memory made him smile. Noble had it even now, filled with the magic he'd found.

Arranging everything but his medicine pouch, which he tucked back under his shirt, in a circle around him, he crossed his legs and settled down. Spreading his arms, palms heavenward, he soaked up the last of the late-fall sun, feeling it pour forth its cleanness into his soul. He hoped and prayed to be purified of all the white man's duplicity, all the little white tricks that blocked his ability to feel the strength of the land.

"Yieii," he chanted, swaying to the music he heard within himself, aware that his strong voice would carry on the wind to the Comanche camp. It wouldn't be long before the tribal police stalked him.

The sense of donning his own skin at long last, of finding his rightful place, overwhelmed him. Feeling the wind ripple his untied hair, he shut his eyes to the men riding out to decide whether he lived or died.

He hadn't long to wait. They didn't try to hide, thundering up the incline, lances and paint ready for an enemy. Johnny's eyes remained shut, his inner peace building as he shed his white skin. He knew that he'd be recognized eventually.

A lance quivered through the air, slicing the ground by his right knee. Unflinching, Johnny waited still.

Finally, hooves stamping nearer and nearer, Johnny spoke in Comanche.

"Brothers, I have come home."

He was free to become a Comanche again. It would take time to fit in, but he'd do it. As he did, he'd ask questions and find Beth, before Noble did. It would be his final act of friendship.

Johnny perched, his nerves tingling with excitement. He had waited too long to come home, and now his reception depended entirely on his passing these first tests.

An arrow shot into the air above his head, winging its way straight above him. Willing himself to ignore its flight path, he knew the chances of its driving into his scalp were slim. They were waiting to see if he would flinch.

The shaft of the arrow twanged inches from his right knee, its head buried in the ground so deeply he knew he'd have been killed instantly if they'd wanted him dead. Still, he maintained his inner peace, knowing the testing would continue.

"Dog, where did you crawl from?" a buck he didn't recognize shouted down at him. "Offal, you nothing, why do you violate our camp?"

Johnny considered the answer carefully. "I said I have come home. Where are my mother's people, the Comanche? I see only boys who should be ashamed of the way they welcome one of their own."

With a leap from a spotted pony, one of them raced

to where Johnny knelt. A chortle of laughter rolled over him, as a hard fist knocked into his shoulder. "You sly one, I should have known. But why are you so changed, is it the white way? We have wondered these many moons what ever became of you after your father's people stole you from us."

Finally, a voice he knew. Fast Cloud, his childhood friend, the one who would know him if they lived to be a hundred years old. Rising to his feet, he held out his arms to his friend, his face painted black, and realized he'd missed his people even more than he'd known. "About time, you silly dove, you must be growing dim of eye not to have known it was me until now."

He was free to become a Comanche once again. It would take some time to feel right about what he was doing, but for now he would revel in their acceptance. At least, he hoped he'd been accepted. A brave wearing a scowl hadn't released his tight grip on the bow yet.

"And who is your friend, Fast Cloud?" Nodding nonchalantly at the scowler, he kept his tone of voice easy.

"Now Comes Thunder, meet Two Hats, as the white eyes call my friend Little Fox. We grew as two together, our grandmothers being sisters. He has been lost to us for many moons. . . ."

"So why does he come back now? What do you want, honored guest?" The sarcasm and animosity punched each word with something only a little less than hate.

Fast Cloud stifled a cluck of disapproval. "Show some manners, my friend. We have much to celebrate. Why, I can tell you of the time Little Fox and I stole into the soldier's hut and—"

Laughing, Johnny put his arm about his friend's shoulders. It was rare to see such hostility when someone had been welcomed as a brother, but for now he would ignore it. "Later, Fast Cloud, after I have eaten some of our good food. It has been too long, and I have much to tell you, and you me."

"Of course, come, you lodge with me, and we will talk into the morning, and—"

"And what of my grandmother? Is she still with us?"

Fast Cloud's face fell. "I don't know how to tell you, cousin, but she left us last winter. If only you'd come sooner, she wanted only to see you before she passed on."

"I thought she'd gone on these many years. She was so old when my mother was killed. . . ."

"But strong, like all of us, and waiting . . ."

Something like a stone hit his stomach. He'd imagined her dead all these years, his memory of her with white hair and dark, crinkled skin dominating any hope she would have been alive.

"Enough for now, Fast Cloud, for I must mourn her properly. Let me take care of my horse, and see how many children you have, and your wife, and your fine friends, and then I will hear more of how she went.''

Fast Cloud, sensing the sudden hurt in Little Fox's voice, picked up the arrow. ''I think the shaft is ruined, Blue Feather.'' Tossing it to the archer, he sprang onto the back of his wiry pony. ''Come, old friend, make haste, we have much to share, and my friends will all want to hear your tales of the white eyes.''

''If he will speak the truth . . . ,'' spat out the archer.

Johnny stared into eyes as black as his own, hatred washing over him. ''I will abstain from making a fool of your friend for your sake, Fast Cloud, but not for long,'' he muttered under his breath.

Fast Cloud cut between them. ''It has been many hard years, Little Fox, and we have learned we must pick our battles. Forgive him for now, for he doesn't know you as I do.''

Picking up his reins, Johnny threw the blanket over the back of his horse. ''For now, then, friend. Remember, though, I never had much patience.'' Johnny knew it would come down to him or the archer, one of these days. It would be the only way he could secure his place once again among his own kind.

Chapter Seven

Noble watched the buffalo hunters, his practiced eyes taking in every stitch of beading, every quill-worked piece, learning from their loot which tribes they'd raided, or traded with. Some of their gear showed fairly new work. The saloon was sparsely populated at this hour, no poker games playing yet. The sawdust floor tracked few boots yet. Noble hoisted the last of his drink and forced himself to within smelling range of the three men.

"Evenin'." He waited for an invitation to sit. The three glared at his intrusion.

"What you be wantin'?" one of the odoriferous men finally said with a grunt.

"Well, seeing as how you've been following the hides, thought you might have heard of a white woman, taken captive awhiles back by the Kiowa." Noble tried to keep the anticipation out of his voice. It would run up the price of any information for sure.

"Ain't heard nothin', boy. Now get outta here and leave us be."

Noble dangled a piece of beadwork on the back of the hide jacket nearest him. "That's Kiowa, mister.

And I got me some gold in my pocket for the man who can tell me something about the woman.''

He knew it was a mistake. But he didn't have time to play games with them, nor did Beth. It had already been much too long for Beth.

''How much?'' Picking his teeth with a thin, lethal knife, the one doing the talking got a sparkle in his eyes.

''Ten dollars. Gold. Now.''

''Let's see it.''

Noble shook his head. ''Not on me.'' At least he'd had common sense enough to stash his traveling money in the small leather pouch hidden under the saddle flap. Made it easier to keep temptation out of the way, hidden like that.

''So get it, boy. Then maybe we'll talk.'' The knife landed tipdown in the table as the thin man hunkered down and rocked back in his creaking chair. He stared directly at Noble for the first time since Noble had approached the table.

''OK, I'll be back. But if you don't have the information I want . . . ''

''Git.'' The heavy smell from the oil lamps in the bar suddenly made Noble feel nauseous. Being inside too long always made him feel cooped up, but the heavy mantle of death that rode these men, aligned with the oppressive odor of the lanterns, suddenly made him careless in his desire to get his business over with. He wanted to get their information and get out of there.

The rush of cold air brought him back to life. Pausing on the planks of the walkway outside the saloon, he gulped in the purity of the night air. Damn the three, they'd probably seen Beth in their trading with the Kiowa. Now they were toying with him like a stray dog being teased with a bone. Part of him was annoyed, the other part didn't give a hoot. He'd get what they had, come hades or high water.

The saddle leather was stiff with cold. Noble warmed his fingers in his mouth before trying the knot in the small pouch. He didn't have much left, he realized as he dug at the knot with his nails. He'd wire the Old Man, get a bank draft sent someplace close. He was still thinking of the Old Man when his hackles rose like a dog about to pounce a skunk.

"What the . . . ?" He spun around as the clear, crisp night air was suddenly saturated with the stink of rotting carcasses. The buffalo hunters ringed him, their thick coats and matted hair making them look, in the pale light cast by the saloon, like bison themselves. A carbine was aimed at his gut.

"Hand it over nice, boy, and you won't get hurt."

"It'll be a cold day in—" Noble inched his hand toward his belt. The twang of a knife reverberated at the toes of his boots. The idiot should have used it right, he thought abstractly. Good way to ruin a blade.

Kicking out at the groin of the nearest man, he knew they'd avoid firing to keep from drawing attention to the theft. A sudden "oomph" let him know he'd connected, as the man doubled up and clutched his privates. A fist shot to his right cheek, just in time to catch him in the temple. Ducking, he rolled under his skittering horse, rising on the balls of his feet on the other side to snatch the rifle from his blanket roll on the cantle. The sting in his left leg surprised him as he jerked the rifle to his shoulder to fire. Shooting recklessly, he wanted to scare them off more than kill them. If he killed them all, he'd never get another chance like this for months.

A kick in the leg from his horse and Noble was flat on his back, watching his horse thunder down the dark street, the buffalo hunters hot-footing it to their shaggy ponies. Quirting their mounts, they raced after the gelding into the dark at the edge of town.

He tried to stand. But something wasn't right, as the leg refused to do what he ordered. Feeling it gingerly, he knew from the warm stickiness on his palm he'd been shot. The knowledge he wouldn't be able to ride for days sickened him. Beth didn't have time for him to be shot, he moaned under his breath to himself.

Wrapping the wound in his bandana, he felt for the other problem, and knew from the mess he encountered that the horse had cracked a bone with the kick. A piece of it protruded from his shin. Good Lord, he wished, why hadn't he stayed out on the range? The anger kept him from feeling the first twinges of pain nagging in the back of his mind.

It wasn't going to be long before the shock wore off

and he felt the full force of his injuries, and he knew it. Clawing his way into the street, he shouted for the barkeep. No one answered his call as he lay in the cold, hoping for the numbness to linger long enough to get the leg set, knowing it couldn't. Drat that horse, he cursed, like a sacred litany—drat, drat, drat.

An old cowhand tumbled from the brightness of the saloon just as Noble felt he was going to lose consciousness.

"Help me," Noble croaked, struggling to hold on to his anger at his stupidity, at the horse, at the buffalo hiders he knew he'd find, someday. The cowboy stared into the dark, as though he expected to find a ghost.

"Down here, blast it," mumbled Noble. "Get yourself down here!" He felt fury rise in him like a tornado, fury at himself, at the cowpoke for staring at the street as though he were waiting for Father Christmas.

This time the man saw Noble. Squatting at the edge of the walk, he poked a finger in Noble's direction. "What's up, friend?"

Noble breathed through the pain. Exhaling slowly, he whispered, "Got shot, busted my leg. Carry me inside, before I freeze to death."

"Heck, son, you need a doctor. Ain't got none in these parts." The cowpoke hunkered down beside Noble. "Yep, seems like you need a good horse doctor," he added as he felt the bone poking through Noble's flesh.

Noble rode the waves of pain, feeling them flush in

the face like clouds from a steam engine. With each puff of agony, he began sinking deeper into the darkness within himself.

"Don't care, just get me out of this street!" Noble managed to mumble.

"Ornery cuss, ain't you?" were the last words Noble heard before the silky blackness covered him completely.

Chapter Eight

"Got me a stranger here."

It was colder than Noble had ever felt, even in the middle of a blizzard. He heard the voice through mists of ice that took his breath away.

"Put him here." Noble tried to remember where he was and who he was, but all he knew was his toes curled with frostbite and his fingers felt gone. The freezing air sapped his strength, and he flopped and jostled like a weak calf on cold ground, helpless to stop it. Wanting to cry out, say something, anything, he knew it was too late for his vocal cords. His lips were locked in a silence he couldn't help but abide by. Then he felt even colder, and the jouncing stopped. He drifted off to sleep. Or death. He didn't care which.

The woman was in her early twenties, the thick red braid hanging down the back of her white flannel night-gown making her appear younger. Clutching a robe to her shoulders, she watched as the cowboy jerked the man's jacket from him. "Careful, Richardson, he might have something broke up top too, a rib or some-thing. Longer he stays out, easier it's gonna be to get that leg set."

"Lordy, Miss Rebecca, I've hauled him all the way out here, and he ain't woke up yet. Don't figger he's gonna do it now."

"I know." She smoothed over her prior sharpness. "It's just harder to handle a man trying to be brave than one who's out cold. I swear, men can be such children sometimes, makes me realize the good Lord knew what he was doing when he decided women should have the babies." Kneeling beside Noble, she gently eased her hands along the fractured leg. "Don't think anything else's busted, just this here doozy. If we can keep it clean, he may have a chance to keep the leg. But it's a long one."

"Got a feeling he's tough. Took on three buffalo hunters all by himself. Don't know what it was about, but they took off after his horse when I come out and saw him lying there. Seemed ornery enough then too."

Rebecca turned up the kerosene lamp, thrusting her arms into the old wool robe. "Get some hot water going, will you, Richardson? Gotta get it clean first, then we'll set it. Think I've got some old boards in the shed, and some extra sheets." She was thinking aloud, her small, heart-shaped face intent on Noble's shallow breathing. "He's not out so far he's going to stay that way long. By any small chance, do you happen to have a bottle of whiskey in that saddlebag of yours?"

"Miss Rebecca, you know me better than that!" Richardson grinned at the suggestion. "Got me two bottles, of course."

The pale yellow light cast by the lamp made her freckles jump out like a child's in sunlight. When she cocked her head to one side, she didn't look over sixteen. "Then get going, cowboy. Time's a-wasting, and I'll need it to clean my hands and the wound."

"Yes, ma'am." Richardson groaned his acquiescence. Trudging out of the cabin, he cursed his ill fortune in finding the unlucky stranger. Miss Rebecca, widow at age nineteen, owner of a small ranch she inherited from her young husband, local midwife, was wooed by every cowhand in the county. But none yet had found favor with her. It was as though the cholera that had taken her husband had taken her joy with him, and she no longer thought of herself as young. Richardson had hoped she'd at least have one little drink with him in recognition of his samaritanism.

Gently easing Noble out of his shirt, she was surprised at how young he looked. Normally, weather and woes etched lines far beyond the years on a man's face, and Noble had at first seemed quite a bit older. Running her fingers through his pants pockets, she found only a hanky, well worn and dirty, and a few coins. There was no sign of who this man could be, this man whose leg—and probably livelihood—rested in her care.

"Richardson," she shouted out, hoping he'd hear her before returning with the liquor, "bring in the gun you found with him. Maybe," she continued to herself, "just maybe he's put his name somewhere on the gun. Stranger, hate like hell to have you die on me and have no name for the marker." It's important, she thought, that every marker have a name. She'd seen so many, so often, tiny crosses on windswept hills, and every time, she'd insisted that there be a name, a way of saying that this person, this child, had been here, even if not for very long. It may be just a stopping place to better and higher things, Lord, but someone should know you've been here.

Richardson bustled in, carrying more firewood and Noble's rifle. "Anything else, Miss Rebecca?"

"Just get yourself cleaned up. I may need your help getting this bone back where it belongs." The lines at the corners of her deep blue eyes were deeper at times like this, as she sat thinking of what she had to do. She'd done it so often, she thought, ever since she was a child on her father's place, piecing men back together because they seemed to stay calmer when she did it, birthing the breech colts, nursing the dogs when they ate a bad prairie dog. A body'd think she could do it in her sleep, but no two broken bones were ever the same. It was like other women took pride in their straight quilt lines and pretty stitches, she took pride in the straight and strong bones she put back into place.

Fetching her sewing basket, she held an embroidery needle to the flames of the fireplace. Her white thread already knotted, she slipped the point into the collar of her bedrobe, and shoved the sleeves behind her elbows. "Here, Richardson, pour it over my hands. Then do yours. We better get moving."

Richardson hung the water over the fire and poured some of his whiskey over her waiting hands. "Seems like a waste of good liquor, Miss Rebecca. Reckon we might sample just a bit, to fortify ourselves for the task ahead?" One look from her, and he quickly poured the remainder on his hands, stashing the bottle back in his saddlebags. "Yes, ma'am, ready when you are."

Holding the leg still for her, he watched as Rebecca positioned the protruding bone and pushed. The grating sound it made caught at his throat, but Rebecca listened intently, probing the wound with her fingers until she was certain it was straight.

"Good, Richardson, so far he's still out of it. Now pour some of that good liquor right here"—she gestured at the open wound—"and bring me the water." Quickly she began to sew the leg, suturing the wound with small stitches worthy of a ball gown. Dipping her hands in the water, she washed off the blood and ripped open some cotton sheets. Stanching the blood from the gash with a bit of sheet, she frowned as Noble began to mutter. "Not now, cowboy, you stay under awhile longer," she whispered. She still had to set the splints before he came to.

Richardson watched from a corner as Rebecca measured and cut at the boards he'd fetched from the shed, as careful as though she were making a cradle. Finally satisfied, she bound the leg in the confines of the brace and stepped back to admire her handiwork.

"Not too bad, Richardson, not at all." Without hesitation, she turned to the side wound. It had been clear, from the lack of pink foam at his mouth, that the bullet missed the lungs. Probing behind him with her long fingers, she found where the bullet had passed through the flesh and muscle, missing the vital organs. Reaching for the bottle, she accepted it from Frank's reluctant hands. Dousing the wound liberally, she tossed Frank a half-smile.

''No, ma'am.'' He wished she'd call him Frank sometimes. But it was as though all the men who'd paid her court were destined to be nothing more than friends, and never first-name friends at that.

''Think the Lazy Y can put him up in the bunkhouse when I can get him there?''

''I'll ask the boss. More 'un likely.'' Rebecca Fairholm had patched together so many men at the Lazy Y, the boss would do anything she asked. Besides that, he was sweet on her himself. Richardson sighed. At least he'd see her if she came to check on the stranger.

''What about the gun. Anything on it? Haven't found a clue in his pockets.''

Richardson settled onto a hard wooden rocker in front of the fire and ran his fingers over the smooth, well-oiled barrel of the rifle. ''Good-lookin' weapon. Not new.''

Rebecca's braid shifted over her shoulder as she leaned beside him to look. ''Expensive. Even used. Not your ordinary coyote rifle. Suppose he stole it?''

''He sure don't look well heeled, that's for sure. But

somehow, he don't look the type to take nothing that ain't his. Don't ask me why.'' Richardson's fingers lingered over the butt.

"Here it is." Holding the base of the rifle to the firelight, he stared at the small silver filigree. "I'll be danged. Looks like a piece of ladies' jewelry."

"I know what it is." Rebecca traced the outline with a fingertip. "It's initials. *N* and *M*. Just the two."

They both stared at Noble, who was beginning to toss on the cot. Rebecca hurried to his side, pressing her palm to his forehead. "Don't look like much, stranger. But at least you've got good taste in rifles." Propping the quilt up on the planks she hadn't used for the splint, she adjusted it to keep the weight off the leg. "Now we at least can put *NM* on your marker," she mumbled to herself.

She'd seen too much death. She wanted this one to live, although the chance for gangrene was huge. Don't think about it, she told herself. Just don't think about it.

"Richardson, can I offer you a blanket? Or do you feel you've gotta ride on?"

"Reckon I'd better get back, Miss Rebecca. Tell the boss we may have a guest. Get Rusty some dinner."

"Rusty, of course. Why didn't you put him up in the shed? I've got some hay...."

"No need, Miss Rebecca, he's stood worse weather." Just like her, he thought, thinking even of a horse's comfort. How he wished she'd take the same thought for him.

She stood briefly in the door as he mounted, the light from the fire framing her like angel wings. "Night, Richardson, and thanks for your help."

"Name's Frank, Miss Rebecca," he whispered into the night as he reined Rusty toward the Lazy Y.

Chapter Nine

The old woman was a healer. Gradually, it dawned on Beth that the Kiowa came to her with burned hands and swollen insect stings, minor ailments that she poulticed and doctored. The crone didn't have the status of an elite shaman, but she served her people well.

Beth watched her disappear in the early gray light of dawn, returning with a basket filled with grasses and roots. Each morning the woman refilled her apothecary, as though preparing for the day's small ills and injuries.

The nights were getting colder. She huddled as close as she could to the tepee, hoping for shelter within when it became so cold she couldn't stand it. So far, she'd been left alone, small handfuls of food from the old woman her only sustenance. If she'd had the nerve to risk her nonperson status, she'd have followed the woman one morning, to see what she collected. They both ate from the basket's bounty.

Beth listened intently as the Kiowa talked, trying to discern a pattern to their speech that would allow her to speak to them, but so far she'd picked up only a few words, like water, dog, and rain. There'd been no sign of rescue.

One little boy had hung around her, staring for hours at a time. His thick, dark hair hung in his eyes, and she longed to reach out to give his face a wipe and clean some of the mess from his cheeks. Always watchful, he'd stay just beyond her reach, a stick or child-sized boy doll dangling from a fist. She wondered if he stalked her like prey, or had just never seen a white woman before.

It seemed as though her antics at the beginning of her captivity had secured her a permanent place as the tribe's resident crazy woman. Now she longed for companionship, someone to say words she could understand. She wanted to bathe, brush her hair, and sleep on one of the soft hides they piled in their tepees. She smiled daily at the tiny boy, resisting the urge to grab him in a huge hug. One day, he gave her a timid grin in return, and her heart soared with joy. She felt as though she could survive if at least one human being acknowledged her existence. To the hag, Beth was a nonentity, like an old dog that required some care but didn't really matter.

They reached the main tribe late one morning. Beth's heart pounded as she heard the yips and yells from the front of the column. Even the old woman smiled at nothing, giving Beth another poke in the ribs to hurry her on. Beth knew her chances for escape had fallen like a stone in an avalanche.

The crone had Beth drop her burden at the edge of a much larger camp. Jabbering, she motioned for Beth to set up the tepee, while she hurried away. Beth struggled with the poles, praying she'd be able to do at least some of the hard job before the crone reappeared to stab her in the ribs again with the sharp stick she used regularly.

That night the hag reappeared to give Beth a small scold and grab something from one of the carefully laced parfleches. Beth watched her smooth out a beautiful white dress made of some sort of skin, decorated with trade beads and embroidery. The squaw donned the garment, ignoring Beth. Suddenly, Beth realized it was a celebration, and the woman was putting on her best finery.

She was afraid to get too close to the crowd gathering in the center of the camp. Something warned her she was still vulnerable, despite her slave status.

As night fell and deepened, the chant of the women and the beat of drums grew more insistent. Wrapping her forearms tightly to her head, she tried to force the sounds to go away. She knew what they were doing. They celebrated killing her people and taking the beef.

Staring at the star-laden autumn sky, she wished she had the courage to strike out. Tonight would be, in all likelihood, her last chance to escape. If only she knew which way to go! If only she had proper clothing, a horse, some supplies!

She thought briefly of stealing what little the old

woman had stored in the parfleches, but gave it up as useless. There was barely enough for the two of them to eat daily, even when the woman had a busy morning at her gathering. There was no way Beth could manage to steal a horse; she'd only get caught and probably dragged to the celebration as part of the party. Worst of all, she wasn't sure which way was home.

The next morning the village was slow to awaken. Even the dogs kept quiet. She huddled alone, waiting for food. The old woman forgot her until that night. Beth felt hate slowly growing in her like an ember that needed to be coaxed. She nursed it carefully.

Beth took to wandering the compound. Eventually, she fashioned together enough of her old clothes and scraps of hide the old woman discarded to keep herself warmer than she had been. It was only by weaving together reeds she found by the riverbank that she pieced together a shelter for herself. With the help of some fallen logs and her crude mats, she made a nest for herself.

One day the crone staked out a cowhide skinned from one of the purloined beeves. Beth watched, fascinated, as the woman scraped the skin tirelessly, honing away at the fat and tissue with a sharp rock. The crone's thin arms moved with the rhythm of a paddle wheel, and Beth found herself mesmerized by the work. The hide sat out in the sun all that day; the next dawn, the crone flipped it to work on the side with hair.

Beth found a rock, selecting it carefully. It was no-where near as sharp or easy to hold as the old woman's, but she dared to touch the hide with it. The crone paused, seeming to see Beth for the first time. Rocking back on her heels, she stared at Beth's rock. For a moment, the woman seemed to believe Beth was going to hit her with the rock.

Then, wrapping her birdlike talons around Beth's wrists, she guided Beth's hands, scraping at the tough hair with short jerks. Beth felt the power in the old woman's arms, and was shocked at how weak she felt herself. Still, Beth pressed the rock into the hide, trying to emulate the swift jerking action that removed tufts of hair.

They worked for hours on the hide, wetting it down, smoking it, rescraping it yet again. Beth watched with some pride as the stiff piece of rawhide slowly softened into a dark piece of leather. The old woman seemed to ignore Beth's efforts, grunting now and then when she had to rework a spot Beth hadn't completed to her satisfaction.

Beth's voice grew softer. She spoke to herself when she was alone at night, and found a lump welled in her craw if she tried to raise her tone. The old woman still ignored her, except when handing her a few bits of food. Beth grew bolder, following her in the days when she gathered herbs and ground them for poultices. Occasionally, Beth would hold the basket for the woman as she sliced away at some root. Even yet, no one spoke directly to Beth. She was still not recognized as a person.

Yet daily she felt compelled to walk among the Kiowa, to let them know she was still there, still alive. All thoughts of running were forgotten, she didn't know where she was or how to get home. As long as the woman gave her small handouts and left her alone, she hoped the day was growing closer when rescue was at hand. The Army, her father especially, was bound to come looking for her. If the Army didn't, she knew Noble would, as soon as he was able. The longer she stayed in one place, the better her chances of being found.

Watching the women filing out in the mornings with baskets on their hips, she reasoned they were stocking up food for the coming winter. After they returned, she watched as they spread berries and wild fruit on rocks in the sun, pulverizing nuts and roots with wooden mallets after the fruit had already dried. The concoction was then packed into leather satchels. As the days grew shorter and the women worked harder to dry the meat and store the fruit, she felt a chill settle upon her that had nothing to do with winter. She would die if she didn't have food and shelter from the coming cold. A Kansas winter could kill livestock, and she wasn't even as hardy as livestock.

The small boy began following her from her shelter as she made her rounds of the camp. The dogs too trailed behind them, as though a parade had come to town. Now and then she imagined the picture they presented, and would laugh aloud. But the little boy would run from her in a flurry of dust and barking dogs when she laughed, so she stopped. He was her only friend, and she couldn't afford to lose him. Gradually, he would sit at her feet as she collected what small, unripe berries had been left by the women on their morning rounds, and he would play in the dirt with rocks and his stick.

No one seemed upset that he trailed her like a lost lamb. He ate from anyone's meal pot, and she saw several men and women give him affectionate cuffs on the shoulder as he darted in and out of different lodges. Gradually, she realized that all the children ran wild, playing boisterous games in packs that reminded her of wild kittens. This one tiny boy, about five years old she guessed, had cut away from the others, and she wasn't sure why. One day, she knew.

An older girl, swaggering like a doxy, flounced up to Beth from across the camp where a gaggle of girls had been shrieking in play. About eight or nine years old, she carried something clenched in her fists as she hipped her way to where Beth sat. Elizabeth, plaiting reeds to make a container for water such as she'd seen other women carry, had paid little attention. Her position as an unseen ghost in the camp was secure by now. Only this time it was different, and the girl planted her feet squarely before Elizabeth, hatred smeared across her young face like a scar.

Startled, Elizabeth looked in the child's dark eyes in time to recognize the danger. One small fist darted out, and a sharp rock smashed into Elizabeth's cheek. Checking her instinct to smack the insolent face not four feet from her, she turned her back instead. She knew from watching the Indians around the forts her father had commanded that children were never struck as a form of discipline, and besides, she had no right to act at all. Retreating into her cloak of insanity, she began softly singing "Onward Christian Soldiers," praying the girl would go away before the crazy white woman became a target. Just as she thought she was safe, another stone sliced into the back of her scalp, and she knew how the woman taken in adultery must have felt before Jesus shamed the crowd.

Ignoring the blood trickling down her face, she turned to stare at the child, hoping to shame her into submission. The girl, giggling malevolently, took aim with yet another rock, but this time dropped it with a startled grunt. Beth wondered what had happened, as another stick flew through the air and struck the girl in the side.

"Yieeei," the tiny boy chortled, pleased with his marksmanship.

Twirling with a screech, the older girl dropped her rocks. An angry spate followed, as the other children ran laughing in circles around the girl with the stones, obviously complimenting Beth's friend on his skill with the bow and arrow. Beth faded from the crowd, walking slowly to her hut, puzzled at the girl's sudden aggression and her rescue by her tiny friend.

Something had shifted in Beth's position in the camp, and her little camp follower, sensing it long before her, had come to her rescue. She crouched in her shelter of reeds, arms hugging her knees, and for the first time since her capture, she sobbed.

Chapter Ten

The waning days of autumn were golden, although winter on the wind made them all edgy. Johnny cut his hair in belated mourning for the grandmother who had died the winter before. He felt himself slipping into the old ways of his early childhood, the ways that somehow felt more right than all the years he'd spent following the Army with his father.

There was a brief spate of warm weather, and the war chief decided they'd raid south. They hoped to find cattle and hunt buffalo. Fast Cloud brought word of the good news to Johnny.

"You may ride my second war horse. He's not as young as my new one, but he's strong and keeps his feet under him."

Johnny itched with turmoil. What if they found a white settlement to take?

"I'd be honored. I would feel more honored if you would take my pistol for use on the raid." Johnny couldn't afford to offend his one friend. His welcome had been casual among many of the tribe, with Blue Feather the only one who was openly hostile. It would seem odd if he didn't find some way to reciprocate his friend's kindness.

"When do we ride?" It wasn't too long until the winter rendezvous with Noble. Hunting parties had been known to stay away a month or more, and he didn't have much time to ask the questions that needed asking.

"Daylight, day after next. I'll see that my woman packs your provisions." Fast Cloud was going out of his way to include Johnny, and Johnny knew it. It was to be a test, both for himself and his old friend.

"I'll make my medicine now, and be ready to ride."

The bustle about the camp was contagious. It was as though this last chance for glory meant more than a final raid before the winter cold. Johnny wondered if its importance had to do with his presence, and a feeling that he might have brought bad luck—or good luck—to his Comanche family.

A gambling game of bones was feverishly concluding on a smooth spot of ground not far from where Fast Cloud had left him. Johnny ambled over, intent on the game. Chatter centered on the throw, on who had wagered what. Blue Feather materialized behind Johnny.

"Do you wager?" The question was more of an insult. Blue Feather's voice was louder than necessary for Johnny to hear him.

Johnny shrugged. "When the stakes are worth it. Why?" He'd automatically given himself an out.

"Shall we wager on the raid? I hear you ride with us."

Johnny sensed the danger, knew it was unavoidable. "I ride, yes."

"Will you count coup, take scalps?" Blue Feather's voice was almost a snarl, as though Johnny couldn't undertake such glories.

"We will see, won't we?" Johnny folded his arms, rocking back. He tried to keep his tone light.

"Then I place a wager, with all here to witness. Whoever counts more coups, takes more scalps, keeps my war pony and your rifle—the one which fires each time you move the handle. I have seen such a rifle among some whites we attacked, and it fires faster than any rifle I have seen. You must have been a mighty man among the whites."

The insult was clear, the nuance plain. Blue Feather had labeled Johnny a white man who used the newest in rifles against the Indian. The Yellow Boy Winchester was his private joy, the gift he'd given himself for staying so long in the scouts. It was the only thing of real value he owned that wasn't issued by the U.S. Army.

"Not so mighty a man. But why would you wish to wager at all, my friend? Aren't we after cattle, food for the winter to take the place of the buffalo, which are growing scarcer?" He knew he had Blue Feather. Little Fox had made it clear that this raid was for hunting and getting cattle, horses, and goods.

"Are you afraid to kill your own kind, Little Fox?" Blue Feather's voice was menacingly low.

"I do not kill the Comanche, no." Johnny crawled with suppressed anticipation. The moment was ripe for Blue Feather to make his move.

Fast Cloud shoved through the gathering crowd to his side. "You try to insult my friend, you insult me, Blue Feather."

Johnny forced his eyes to his friend. "I make my own enemies, Fast Cloud."

His friend shrugged, worriedly giving him a good-natured jostle. "Not among the Comanche, Little Fox. Ignore Blue Feather, he covets your rifle and is afraid I will win it from you first. Come, my woman has questions as to what you wish to carry with you, and I will have no peace in my lodge until they are answered."

Johnny twisted a smile at Blue Feather. "You see, my friend claims the right to wager first for my rifle. I cannot offend him." Twisting, he led the way to Fast Cloud's lodge. The murmurs followed them both.

Fast Cloud held the door of the lodge for Johnny, one hand on his back as he bent to enter. The pressure of his friend's hand stopped him as he half-stooped. "Do you mean to kill the white eyes, if we come upon them?"

"So you too wonder about me? Do I bring such shame to this tribe?"

"It's not that I wonder. But your father was a blue-coat. It must be hard to hate your father's kind."

"Not so hard." Johnny meant it. "And it doesn't take hate to kill." He realized he meant what he said. He stooped farther, escaping his friend's hand. Fast Cloud's wife continued her work, politeness causing her to act deaf to their conversation. Johnny nodded politely to her. Her eyes averted, she folded the garment on her lap and rocked from her heels to her feet.

"I will be honored to pack your horse for the raid, friend of my husband."

Johnny smiled, taking a seat on the buffalo hides stacked around the rim of the floor. "Whatever you think is proper and good medicine, wife of Fast Cloud." Glancing around the lodge, he saw Fast Cloud's medicine bundle and buffalo club hanging in their sacred place. The white beaded eyes of the horsehair buffalo head on the end of the club seemed to stare at him.

"What must I do, my friend, to become a member of the Club Men?" The power of the position was formidable. But he hadn't been around through the years of advancing from one honorary society to the next. He would have to skip those steps to earn a place among the warriors who raced first to the enemy, then back to join the other warriors in a concentrated attack.

Fast Cloud settled beside him. "You must speak with your spirit leader, Little Fox, and ask what you must do. I can't tell you the way."

Johnny knew he was right. It was high time he made the commitment it would take to give him back his birthright, all of it. He felt the lack within himself. He hadn't listened to his spirits for many years. If he was ever to be at peace, it had to be made now.

"I will go now, and listen. Come for me when it is time."

Fast Cloud nodded. The enemies they raided would find that the Kiowa had gained a warrior to be truly feared, he had no doubts about it. Blue Feather and the others who murmured about Little Fox would have to swallow their words with dust.

Chapter Eleven

Noble struggled to sit up, and vomited. Flopping back with a groan, he waited for the dizziness and the pounding in his temples to subside. They didn't. "Good Lord Almighty," he croaked, "will someone get me a glass of water?"

The redheaded angel he'd been dreaming about materialized over him. Stretching his shaking hand as far as he could reach, he fingered the thick braid on her shoulder. "So I'm still here, huh? Thought you met me at the pearly gates hours ago."

"More like days." She held the tin dipper to his cracked lips. "Been calling me Elizabeth. Just to set the record straight, though, name's Rebecca. Now how about a moniker for you, cowboy?"

He thought a minute. "Seems to me, it's Noble McFarland. Sounds good, anyway. Guess it'll all come back to me one of these days. How bad am I?"

"Think we saved the leg. No infection so far. Everything's mending nicely, thank you very much, and I do believe you might even walk again."

Noble winced. "How about ride? I got places to go, now."

Lowering the dipper to her side, she shrugged. "We'll have to wait and see. You look like a tough one to me."

Scraping his palm across his bearded cheeks, Noble winced. "Must look mighty rough, ma'am. Got a razor anywhere?"

She shook her head. "No need to get pretty on my account. You just better keep your head down, Mr. McFarland, until you get to feeling a mite bit steadier." She pointedly mopped up the mess on the floor beside his bed. "Besides, I like the beard. Makes you look older. How old are you, anyway?"

Noble thought for a minute. "Reckon I'm eighteen, or close thereabouts. Why?"

Her freckled face was thoughtful as she wrung the cloth in the wooden bucket. "You mind me some of my late husband. He was about your age when we married. Lost him two years later to a rogue longhorn on a cattle drive."

"I'm sorry." He could think of no other appropriate response.

"Not your doing, Noble McFarland. Now you get some rest while I see about getting some food fixed for a rocky stomach."

"Don't feel like eatin' much." He didn't relish the thought of being sick again. Especially not when he knew what he was doing. "Who's been taking care of me?"

She laughed, low and throaty, as she turned her back

to him. "Who else, you silly man? See anyone else in this cabin?"

"You mean, hrumph, everything? You got no man to help you? I guess you, well—"

"Just me, and now and then Frank Richardson. He brought you here, helped me change your bandages, held you down a couple of times. Good man, Frank. You oughta thank him and your lucky stars he found you. You'd a-froze to death right fast, quick as you were losing blood."

Noble searched his memory, but it was just out of reach. "Don't remember anything, to be truthful. But if you'll point him out, I'll give my thanks."

"It'll come back. You've been out a long time, about five days. Delirious some of it, by your talkin'. Fever'll jelly your brains some." She laughed as she stirred the pot over the iron cookstove. "Got some beef broth here, should do the trick."

The thought repulsed him. "Guess I'll give it a try, you say so."

She sat on the edge of the cot, her blue gingham dress spread on the quilt that covered him. Leaning over, she braced his head under the crook of her elbow and lifted him. He felt weak as a newborn pup, all quivering.

"Now, sip," she commanded, holding the blue mug to his lips. "It's not too hot, and you've gotta start sometime ifn' you want your strength back."

Gagging on the first mouthful, he tried to swallow.

Her warm breast leaned against his arm, and he was aware of how strong she was as she raised him higher to drink. Somewhere in his memory, he thought of a woman who had held him close and comforting, and he struggled to see her face.

"Mother."

Rebecca paused with the cup. "Not hardly, Mr. McFarland. I'm barely three years your elder."

"No, not what I meant," he stumbled. "I was just remembering someone, and suddenly I knew who it was, is all."

"Good sign." She smiled at him as he took another sip. "Things coming back to you so fast, you'll be outta bed in no time."

"Hope so. Got a feeling I need to be riding, that someone's waiting for me."

"Well, they'd best wait a good sight longer. You're still on the mend, Mr. McFarland, and I don't let my patients go until I think they're ready. I'm the doctor in these here parts, and what I say goes!"

He laughed at her lecture, given with a smile, and groaned as the effort made his head split open again. Quickly she lowered him down again.

"That'll do for now. I'll leave the cup here, by your right hand, and whenever you feel able, you take a drink. I'll be outside within earshot, if you need me."

Watching her don a man's buffalo jacket, hide side in, he was struck by her tiny size. Having just felt the muscles in her arms, he knew she was strong as an ox, but so tiny and frail-looking he wondered how she'd cared for him. Taking the ax by the door with her, she slipped out quickly.

The silence in the cabin roared in his ears for the first time. Then he heard the sound of wood chips flying, as she went after the woodpile. It made him feel useless and frustrated that he couldn't even feed himself, much less help her with the wood. Pulling himself out of his self-pity, he looked around the cabin for the first time, carefully noting the neatly ironed and starched curtains with little red dots, the cherry bed in one corner with a crazy quilt tucked over the top, and the walnut wardrobe next to it. A handmade rocker, a hand-smoothed table, and two small spindle chairs clustered about the fireplace, while the cookstove dominated a wall of its own. He could see the door leading to the cold pantry, and a small lean-to off the front part of the pantry. He guessed she must have a hired hand who stayed in the lean-to.

A round daguerreotype, framed and matted by red ribbon, hung just over his bed. Looking up at it from his pillow, he could tell the man looked stiff and awkward in the suit, while the woman proudly rested her hand on his shoulder as her fine dress train swirled about both their feet. He couldn't tell if the woman was Rebecca, just that both of them looked mighty young.

The split oak floor had been sanded and polished to within an inch of its life, as had everything else in the small room. Fingering the woolen quilt covering him, Noble suddenly realized that he was in just his longjohns. His shock was momentary, however, as he moved his hand experimentally over himself to assess the damage to his body. The throbbing he'd been experiencing as he lay awake was nothing compared to the pain that riveted through him as he felt his side, his arm, and his leg. He thanked God he could still feel them.

It took all his strength to raise himself on one elbow. He'd been down too long. He felt like a horse with colic, and knew it would be better for him in the long run if he could just get his feet under him. The pain pulsed through every inch of him as he wiggled his good leg to the floor. Gently pulling the leg in the splint beside it, he dug his fingers into the mattress ticking as he steeled himself to stand.

The door flopped open on its leather hinges. Throwing the firewood down, Rebecca raced to his side, her face flushed and a scowl worthy of a schoolmistress between her eyes. "What the blue blazes you think you're doing, Noble McFarland? Get yourself back in bed this instant, or I'll put you back there myself, and I mean *now!*" Hands on her hips, arms akimbo, she stared him down like a first sergeant taking down a green recruit.

"But Rebecca," he began to protest.

"Don't 'but' me, mister. I set the sixty million broken pieces in that leg, and I know just how fragile it is, and if you put any weight on it, I'll personally pull it off you and beat you on the head with it!''

He had to laugh, although it hurt even more. ''Yes, ma'am.'' His voice was meek, but he knew he wasn't fooling her. She knew he'd try again.

Pulling the quilt over him, she clucked under her breath like a mother hen scolding a chick. ''Men, so stupid sometimes, can't stay in bed, just like a child, no common sense, how they survive without women is beyond me . . . '' were just a few of her mutterings he caught. He thought perhaps silence was the best he could do for the moment.

Her eyes were wonderfully blue as she leaned close to make sure he got her meaning. ''If you don't stay in this bed, I'll tie you down. And I make a mean knot, mister, you'll have to be some kind of magic man to get out of it, so you stay put. Hear?''

''I hear.'' The effort to defy her had cost him. Still, he knew he'd have to try again, because he had to keep going. He wasn't sure why quite yet, but the feeling was urgent like the need to drink and eat and scratch. He closed his eyes and waited for an answer. Just as he drifted off into a troubled sleep, he saw her again, the girl with the dark blond hair who'd been part of his dreams with Rebecca. Still faceless, she wore blue like Rebecca, and was turned half away from him. He wanted to call out to her, when he felt a cool hand on his forehead.

"Sleep, Noble McFarland. Don't dream, sleep." Clasping her wrist with his bony fingers, he held her hand until the dream was gone, and he was deeply asleep.

Chapter Twelve

Beth waited and waited, the sky leaden, everyone scurrying about like squirrels readying for winter. Then, one gray afternoon, a faint smatter of wetness stuck to her eyelid, and she knew the snows had come. Even her tiny friend, the boy with the bow and arrow, had disappeared. Her tatters were now covered with a woven grass cape fashioned with bleeding fingers, but the cold cut her to the bone anyway. She felt abandoned as the days faded into endless gray hatred, hatred for the Kiowa for taking her, for her family for not finding her, hatred of herself for having wanted so desperately to live that she would have done anything. She lived and breathed hatred, and wondered if she would be consumed by it before the cold got her.

One day the old woman emerged from the tattered tepee in her white dress, its shells and beads looking strangely summerlike in the early winter dawn. Gathering up her few baskets and parfleches, she filled them with her few tools, including her knives, and the extra herbs. Beth wondered if she were about to perform a ceremony, when she watched the crone shuffle to tepee after tepee, leaving her meager belongings at their doors. Beth hugged her few bits of reed shelter to her, and wondered if she should follow. But the cold bit into what was left of her leather boots, filled with holes. She watched as the hag stumbled out of the camp, her pale dress shining softly in the pale morning light.

She must have dozed, because when she next awoke, the gifts the woman had left at each door had disappeared. The regular bustle of the women had begun; the men lounged about as they were want to do in this time of plenty. Many of the cattle still remained, Beth had noted. The women had spent weeks slaughtering one beef after another, using every possible piece of the animal for something. Not even the blood clots were allowed to go to waste. Beth wondered how the puddinglike stew tasted, made over the campfires.

Her hunger was so deep, anything would have been a Turkish delight to her starved taste buds. Huge clumps of meat had been smoked, sausages made from the guts, bones sharpened for awls. The skin given the old woman had been from a smaller, older cow, one that the other women evidently felt safe in giving to the crone. The old woman had made herself moccasins and patches for the tepee from the leather, saving every scrap she hadn't already stitched.

Beth watched the bustle of the camp all that day from her hiding place in the reed shelter. No one came to the tepee for treatment of a small wound. That night, Beth searched anxiously in the shadows for the old woman to return. The fire had long since slipped into embers, and Beth hunted about the tepee for the small supply of wood the woman kept. Only a few pieces were left. The woman usually gathered wood in the mornings when she collected her herbs. Beth fed the fire, twig by twig. Cold and hunger were her constant enemies. She fed them, and her hatred, with the fire.

The old woman didn't come back, not the next day, nor the next. Beth slipped into the tepee at night. None of the woman's old buffalo hides were left. Beth realized she must have given those away also.

No food found its way to her feet these bitter days. She could see each bone and vein in her wrist, and no longer cared if she ate. It would be easier to huddle in her shelter and wait for a white blanket to lull her to sleep for the final time. Sometimes she slept the night and day through, a dark, dreamless sleep that left her feeling exhausted.

After one too many of the sleeping bouts, she forced herself to rise, struggling up on legs she could barely feel. She staggered drunkenly about the camp. A thin layer of frost covered the packed, grassless ground like a spangled skirt, and for a second she was dancing at a cotillion, her crinolines swirling to music as night stars shone through the French doors. But her cracked and bleeding toes stubbed a pile of bones, hidden by the camp dogs, and she stopped, forcing herself to remember where she was. And her hatred.

At first the silence about her was startling. She feared she'd lost her hearing since the old woman had gone, and she had become nothing more than a castoff among the tribe. Sometimes she wondered if she wouldn't have been better off as someone else's slave, fed by scraps she fought for, rather than the faceless status her craziness had stamped upon her. Leaning into the wind, she strained to hear one other sound, one human voice, just so she could scream it back.

She chewed bones left by the dogs, gnawed at edges of the old leather tepee. The fields that had yielded their bounty to the women all that fall were barren. She fed the fire what dry grasses she could collect, and drank icy water from the river's edge. She shut her eyes as she drank, so she wouldn't chance to catch her reflection. She knew the image wouldn't be her, the real Beth. That Beth was dead. It just remained for her body to realize it and catch up. If the winter didn't kill her first, hatred would do the job in the end. She despised herself for living, her family for not finding her, and the Kiowa for forcing her into her present estate.

Several months must have passed—she'd seen two moons when one cold winter evening, a low chant drifted her way. Relieved, she chapped her rough hands together with glee, sure in her knowledge that she hadn't yet passed into true madness. Anxious for death, yet eager for human contact, she stumbled on, following the sounds like a rat after the pied piper. She didn't care if she was being led to her death. The sound reverberated from one of the fanciest, largest tepees.

She crept to its edge, oblivious to the cold ground burning through her meager clothing.

The warmth inside the tepee kept the ice from caking the hides. Recognizing the designs skillfully drawn on the outside as symbols of one of the most important families, she hesitated. The low, plaintive chant called her inward, like iron to a magnet. Slipping around the side, she slithered one hand under an edge, and lifted the hide high enough to see the circle of men, surrounded by women.

The gyrations of the medicine man in the middle of the tepee increased in intensity. Fascinated, she found herself craving to rise and dance with the medicine man, her hands echoing each gesture he made. His garish body paint, the thick, sweet odor from the fire, the frantic whirling, all attacked her senses. For a second, she felt herself in the presence of the Devil himself.

The woman kneeling before her shifted slightly, and Beth saw more clearly. A small, motionless form lay deep within the folds of many buffalo blankets. Something about the medicine man's next series of chants alarmed her, and she knew death was the enemy, not the medicine man. Whoever lay in the bed was going to live or die before the chant was over; she knew that to be the truth as surely as she knew she was going to have to chose to live or die within the next few minutes.

A tiny moan leaked from the mounds of hides, and the medicine man renewed the fervor of his cries. An old man knelt quietly beside the bed and stroked the face of the patient. It was then that Beth recognized him. The tiny figure, bow drawn at her tormentors a few weeks ago, appeared before her as though it were the moment of her torture. Oblivious to her own safety, Beth scrambled back from under the tepee and raced for the door flap. Somehow, she had to save the child, her only friend, her salvation.

Howls of horror, hands flailing, arms shoving her, keeping her away from the boy—she ignored them all in her scramble to his side. They couldn't keep her from the small figure. It was her place to be there, she tried to tell them with her eyes. She felt their shock and disgust at her presence.

An old man, the one she knew as the most revered of their leaders, stared at her with eyes like her father's when she would startle him out of a dream. She knew she was right to do it. Kneeling beside the boy, she felt rather than heard the hubbub cease. Her eyes locked into the old chief's, and for a second, she knew every question had been asked and answered, and permission given, as well as much forgiven. There was a reason she still lived.

She felt her love rise like a powerful weapon, destroying the hate she'd cultivated. She no longer felt herself a superior being to these savages. All of her education, her manners, her condescension vanished before the strength of the love she felt for the child, and she let the venom go from her. The apathy and self-disgust melted with it. It was useless to her, to him, to anyone, and she felt as though a metal band had snapped from her neck, freeing her at long last.

Ruffling her fingers through the boy's hair, she felt the iciness of his scalp. Lord, she prayed, don't let me be too late. Scooping him up in her arms, she sensed the medicine man's anger, and ignored it. The old chief silenced him with one word. Gradually, everyone pulled back, except the old man, and she was alone, cradling the child to her bosom, his face pressed against her grass cape.

"Little one," she said softly, running a finger down his cold cheek. "Little one, I love you." She knew it was true.

Father, help me, she prayed. *You love even the sparrows, please, please, spare this one little boy who has been my strength. He means as much to me as he does to you, so please, please, Lord . . .*

She knew what to do. Slowly, out loud, her face suddenly shining with hope, joy, and love, she began the words she'd been unable to remember for long now.

"Our Father, who art in heaven,
Hallowed be Thy name . . . "

For the first time, in speaking the words aloud, she knew how the disciples must have felt when Jesus taught them the prayer. Savoring the words, her eyes shut so she could see the prayer before her. She truly felt the kingdom, the power, the majesty, and the glory, and the surety that His kingdom had come to earth, to her, to the boy she loved as she'd loved only her brother before. All the hatred and despair swept from her like dirt into the dustbin, and she felt pure, unadulterated love, lifting and sustaining her and the child.

The boy coughed, and opened one eye. A small fist rubbed the other lid. She smiled at him as her heart overflowed with gratitude. She knew now the reason she'd been captured and why she'd been permitted to live. She was a stronger person for it. She placed her forefinger in his fist, and shook his hand.

"Well, my little friend, it's about time. I've missed you."

He smiled and snuggled deeply in her arms, calling out in a clear, strong voice. She recognized the words. Food. He was hungry.

Tears streamed down her cheeks as she handed him to the old chief, who waited with arms outstretched. One tear glistened at the corner of his eye as she tucked a robe about the boy while he held him. Touching the tear with a fingertip, she smiled deeply into his eyes, and saw only love. She said their word for "chief" and the language felt like her own.

Hands passed a gourd to the chief. Taking it, he held it out to Beth, gesturing for her to feed the boy. Kneeling, she lifted the vessel to the child's lips as he slurped hungrily. The chief grinned, first at the child, then at Beth, and snapped a command. Another gourd appeared. Holding it to Beth, he commanded her to eat. She took a sip.

It didn't matter what it was, she was grateful. So grateful, in fact, that she knew she'd never again be capable of hatred.

The name came to her. She'd heard the child call the chief by it, racing to him whenever he could, ignoring the women who scolded, as he trampled through the middle of their work. It was "grandfather." She repeated it aloud.

The chief nodded his assent, his eyes still on the child's face as he drank from the gourd.

"Daughter," he replied.

Chapter Thirteen

Noble grew restless, his leg itchy, his wounds aching more and more as they healed. Never, in all his years, had he been in bed more than a day. Rebecca brought him some ancient books, their paper-thin leather covers turning to dust in his hands as he fanned them from cover to cover.

"*Robinson Crusoe*? Where on earth did you dig this up? And a Bible?" He had to admit, his voice sounded querulous even to him.

"Frank Richardson. Brought them over from the ranch. Hope you're a reading kind of man."

"Of course." Unconsciously he bristled. "I read Defoe when I was eleven, maybe twelve." He tossed the book on the quilt, furious with himself for his ill humor.

"I see." Quietly turning, Rebecca shoved her red braid over her shoulder and shrugged into her buffalo coat. "Well, when I get back, you can read me some. Most folks ain't that fancy, and I'd like to hear the story. Frank says it's real humdinger."

"I didn't see Frank. When did he come by?" Noble

was ashamed of his bragging, but still too foul-tempered to admit it.

"Early this morning. Helped me get in some wood, asked about you." Rebecca headed for the door, her slight figure totally enveloped in the hide coat. "Seems like you're right antsy today. Maybe I'll let you sit in the rocker a spell."

Hope must have glowed from every fiber of his being. "When?" He snapped back, reaching to pull the Ohio Star from the bed.

"How about after lunch?" She didn't wait to hear the full extent of his groans before she headed out the door. Reluctantly, he cracked the Defoe, and found himself drifting away into the tale.

The door burst open as a storm of cold air poured in with Rebecca. "We're gonna get a good one," she blustered as she stacked the chopped wood. "Frank'll probably be snowed in, so you'd better make that book last." She watched him cover the opened pages with a corner of the quilt.

"Sorry. I'll start over for you. . . . "

"Better had." She shrugged out of the coat, and once again Noble wondered at her seeming frailty in contrast to the strength of her will.

"I've been thinking. You said you read that book before, when you were a kid. Try thinking back, and see if that doesn't help your memory. Sometimes, you can remember things that happened a long time ago a lot easier than what you had for dinner yesterday."

"Beans and salt pork."

"Too easy, silly. We've had that every night this week." She reached for her diary, which Noble knew contained her notes about every birth she'd attended as midwife. "I remember real well the first Clancy baby I delivered, and that was well nigh four years ago. I'm not so clear about the second one, and I'll probably have to read in here to remember the name of the third, and it's not due for another month." She paused to read her scrawl, a smile on her face.

"You and your husband, you ever have any . . . children, that is?"

The smile faded slightly. "No. Wish we had— would have made losing him a mite easier."

Noble searched for some way to ease the melancholy that had settled upon her. "Those love apples you grow, over there by the window, you ever eat one?"

Snapping the diary shut, Rebecca shoved it back on the mantel over the fireplace. "Land's sake, no. Things are poison."

"No, they're not. Thomas Jefferson used to raise them for eating. Had 'em in a garden in Monticello."

Rebecca pulled the rocker to his bedside. "Noble, that's two things you've remembered this morning, so far. Now try to think how you know that."

In his mind he saw a sudden flash of a sunny room with a polished oak floor, and a blond girl seated beside him as they poured over a huge volume.

''Beth. She showed me the book about Thomas Jefferson.''

''Who's Beth?'' Rebecca's hands traced the outline of a triangle in the Ohio Star as she leaned forward, her face intense.

Noble shut his eyes, willing himself to see Beth's face, willing his memory to return to him intact, but the essence of the scenario faded completely. ''I can't. Seems like the harder I try, the less I remember. Dang it. Oh, sorry.'' He flopped back on the pillows, anger at the futility of conjuring up the past causing him to curse at Rebecca.

''No need for apologies. So you want to eat one of my love apples?'' She winked, making light of his anger.

''Any time.'' He smiled in return. He knew the blond girl in the schoolroom had to be the same one he saw in his dreams. But all the details eluded him still. Suddenly, a thought occurred to him.

''Do you suppose she's my wife?''

''Who?'' Rebecca stopped in her tracks as she readied a love apple for Noble.

''Beth. That's her name, the woman I have to find. I'm sure of it.''

Rebecca sliced open the tomato, its seeds spilling onto the linen cloth she'd folded beneath it.

''Anything's possible. You'll just have to wait and see.''

Noble sensed a slight coolness in her voice he hadn't heard before.

"You sure you want to eat one of these things?" She passed it to him, its insides pale beside the flame of her hair.

"Eaten 'em before. Won't hurt a body."

"Maybe not the love apple, but love does." She watched him take a bite.

He chewed the piece in silence. Had love hurt her? He'd assumed she'd loved only her dead husband. He didn't dare ask. The answer might be too awkward for them both.

Chapter Fourteen

The air reeked of thunder, crackling with the snap of lightning cutting through the night. Johnny carefully mixed his paints, his dried clays and roots, swirling his forefinger through the colors until they were correct. Swiftly, before he became too white in his thinking again, he smeared his chest with the vermilion and swiped black slashes on his cheeks. Now he was ready. Now he was Comanche. Hands open to heaven, he let his eyelids sink, seeking to fall deep within himself without succumbing to sleep. The war spirit would come to him, he was sure of it. It was time he proved himself to his brothers. Within his mind, he swirled the images around, flashes of war and blood, death and mayhem, the scents of burned flesh, hot metal, and screams of horses. He'd lived through battle before, but this time, the fight he was facing was racing him to the destruction of the life he'd lived since his father had taken him to live in the white man's world. He could never go back.

He pushed the thought of Noble from him. He'd find a way to discover Beth and let Noble know where to find her. It would be difficult now, but he would honor one last promise to the white man.

Dipping his head, he sought the blessing of the Great Spirit. He'd need it. Somehow, he felt dawn just lining the edge of the sky. The hours of his reverie had passed as minutes, and he felt refreshed and emboldened.

There was a polite scratch on his lodge. "My friend, we ride now." Fast Cloud straddled his war pony, casually alert. His extra war horse twitched an ear at the sight of Johnny. A quick smile glimmered across Fast Cloud's face as he caught full sight of the war paint in the pale light of dawn.

"You are ready. Good." Tossing the reins to Johnny, Fast Cloud twirled his horse, guiding him with his knees. Johnny leaped on his steed, exhilaration pouring through his veins like liquor. He could have vaulted a tepee in his thrill. The war gods were with him today, and he itched with the need for glory and coups.

They rode hard, heading for traditional raiding grounds in the south. Johnny sensed the thrill of the chase, the pure joy in feeling the wind fly through his hair in the early dawn. The horses too sensed the anticipation of the moment, snorting and throwing their heads, eager to run flat out across the prairie.

But they kept an orderly march, following the war chief for the raid, Many Trees. The various honorary orders of the men knew their spots, and there was no jostling. Fast Cloud rode with Johnny, a bit behind his level.

"How's he doing?" Fast Cloud nodded to the horse.

Johnny smiled gratefully. "Smooth ride. Many thanks."

"He's steady in a fight."

Johnny suddenly remembered Longwalker, twisted to death on the ground not so many months before. "I knew a horse once, the envy of all who saw him run. I hope someday to steal another like him." As soon as he said it, Johnny knew he was returning to his Indian ways of thinking. There would be honor in stealing a horse as wonderful as Longwalker. It would give him much good medicine.

They rode several days, alert to other war parties, buffalo hunters scrambling for a season's slaughter of buffalo. But they were out for horses, coups, and glory, all of which were scarce that late fall. The weather held, a golden glow that warmed them by the time the sun was high, but couldn't sustain any heat as the orb sank early into the ground. Johnny knew they wouldn't stay out too long, unless the weather held. He'd have to take his chances when he saw them. The fourth night, it rained.

That morning, he sensed it. It had to happen soon. Fast Cloud caught him grinning.

"What's so funny, my friend?" They were up, ready to ride.

"Nothing I can share, just a feeling. This will be a good day."

"Ah hah!" Fast Cloud understood. He hefted his war shield. "We'll see if your war god speaks clearly today."

The wind picked up as they rode, carrying in it a quiet chill that meant they hadn't much time. Rain from the night before had obscured tracks as they circled back from their rounds. But even the rain couldn't hide what had been found. Word spread quickly. Horses, lots of them. A ranchero with a remuda filled to the brim. Johnny wondered quickly why a ranch would be loaded with horseflesh, then realized they were probably remounts for the Army.

The warriors broke into stride, a steady canter behind their leaders. Each man knew his spot perfectly. Johnny stuck close to Fast Cloud, his hands tight on the reins, trying to hold his war horse back from a dead run. It wouldn't do to pass anyone now; he had to wait for his chance to prove himself.

They slowed to a trot, then a silent walk as they reached a small knoll. No signals were needed to fan them out, as each man chose his spot. Johnny felt his belly tighten, flexed his feet, and hefted his rifle. The air held the last hint of rain. It felt good and clean, and he sucked it in until he felt his lungs hit capacity. *Let me go home with honor,* he prayed. *Let me be a Comanche.*

The sun was barely inching up into the cool of the

late-autumn morning. With the raised hand, they screamed into a gallop. Johnny found himself shrieking a war cry he'd never heard, and knew it came from something deep within himself. The small ranch was still dark as they hit, twirling quirts about the poles of the remuda to topple them. Johnny raced into the midst of the swirling herd of horses, flailing with his feet to drive them out into the open. Flaming arrows sliced into the wooden shack beside the remuda. Johnny slipped with sweat on the back of his horse, his palms greasy with excitement. A mare screamed. Thudding into the side of another horse, Johnny's stumbled, and for a second, he reached out to tumble down with his steed. Jerking upright, the animal dodged to his feet.

A crack slammed into a fence post beside him, and he knew it was no stray shot. Instinctively, he snapped the action on the rifle and shouldered it. The man standing in his long drawers in the opened doorway was a fool. He deserved to die, Johnny flashed as he took aim. The dark-haired man twirled with the hit, rocking into the door.

''Yieeee!'' screamed Fast Cloud, shaking his shield. Grinning from ear to ear, he helped drive the horses into the open, Johnny beside him. There was no need for a scalp, he'd get his share of the horses, and that was worth more to him today than anything else.

Bent low, they quirted the rumps of the remuda until tongues lolled and their breathing rasped. No one had followed. Johnny thought it queer that one man had guard of such a large herd, but then the whites were never prepared. He and Fast Cloud trotted beside each other as the sun grew high, and they felt its warmth on their backs.

"Good shooting, old friend." Fast Cloud patted the pistol Johnny had given him. "You didn't give me a chance."

Johnny knew what he meant. He hadn't been sure Johnny would shoot a white man. Others, trotting by them, gave Johnny a quick cuff of friendship on the shoulder. He'd passed the first test. He still twitched with excitement, the feel of the fast raid coursing through his blood. The white man hadn't stood a chance. If you were that big of a fool, you deserved to die, Johnny thought.

They pushed on, the council that night having decided to take the herd with them as they raided farther south. Such a large coup was a sign that they were to gain even greater glory on this last raid of autumn. Johnny realized that some of the tension at his presence in the tribe had disappeared with the bullet into the white man at the ranch. He chatted with some of Fast Cloud's friends.

"We hear you rode with the white-eye soldiers?" One of them finally made bold enough to question him.

Johnny chose to be honest. "True. I was a scout for the Army."

"Did you kill our people for the white eyes?" The taunting voice came from Blue Feather.

''Would I have returned to the home of my mother if I had?'' Johnny's disdain spilled forth.

Fast Cloud changed the subject. ''Tomorrow we will find even more horses! We have much good medicine with us on this raid!''

There was a general assent, and the interrogation ceased. At least, Johnny mulled to himself, they had asked him outright. Now maybe the whispering behind hands would stop.

Chapter Fifteen

Beth ran her fingers through the boy's long hair. "Settle down, little one, or I'll have to stop telling you my story."

It was the ultimate threat, and usually worked to calm down the child. He was winter-weary, aching to run outdoors and let off steam. But the snows were too deep, and she wanted him safe by her side. Sometimes she forgot he wasn't her son.

"Grandfather says the snows will leave us soon, and then I can—"

"Yes, I know, and your grandfather is very wise, but for now, sit still and let me finish my tale."

The Indians never struck their children. Until they reached the age when they began shouldering some of the responsibilities, they were allowed free rein. The white side of Beth wanted some sterner discipline, but she had to admit that the children, loved and cossetted by all in the camp, were basically well disciplined. She assumed that the underlying discipline had grown from a need to keep the tribe together and safe in time of danger.

The times she thought of home and Noble and their

father were growing fewer. Her position in the tribe had solidified into a position of revered elder sister and healer, and her contentment grew daily. The other women had helped supplement her nonexistent wardrobe with soft skin dresses, fur-lined moccasins, and leggings that came to her hips. Watching the thin curl of smoke wisp its way out the hole of the tepee, she felt herself freed from the paralyzing fears that had almost killed her a few months earlier.

''And so, when my brother was a small boy, he found this fawn, and fed it from his hand, and tamed it, and together they would wander here and there. Everyone knew that if they gave a bit of food to my brother, they had to do the same for his fawn. In fact, I think my brother began to grow spots, and look more and more like his fawn.''

''No!'' shrieked the child. ''Why would he grow spots?''

''Well, they slept together, he and the fawn, you see, and after a while, the spots just started rubbing off.''

''Do you think I could find a fawn?''

''And what would you do with it, little one? Make it fat for the cookpot?'' Grandfather ambled in, his buffalo robe shedding snow as he shook it to the ground. ''We will all be hungry if this keeps up much longer, but it won't, will it, Shaman?'' The last of the cattle had been slaughtered long ago, and they were living off the dried meat.

"You know, my chief, I do not divine the weather, only the hearts of men."

"And that is the best gift of all, Shaman. I have need of you. There is some news I would like to discuss with Shaman alone, my grandson. Do you think you could run to your aunt's, and fetch me some pipe fixings? Be sure and wear your heaviest moccasins."

The child leaped up, scrambling for his robes. "May I stay and visit?" His tone was formal.

"Of course, be as sociable as you can be. That is only good manners. Perhaps you can tell your aunt the shaman's tale of her brother."

The child's eyes lit up. "May I have your permission to tell your story, my shaman?" It was rude to retell someone else's story, but a great privilege to be given permission to do to do so.

"Of course. Just make sure you don't tell her the part of the story where my brother was very bad."

"I won't." Happy as a tick on a dog, the child scurried out into the snow.

"The young. It is wonderful how time is for them nothing."

"Yes, Chief. But for this one, I fear we will soon have a boy sick with inactivity if we can't think of more things to keep him occupied. Would you object if I taught him how to read and write the white man's language?"

She knew it was a gamble, because it was a reminder that she wasn't really one of them.

"Do you think he will need this knowledge, Daughter? I would prefer he learned the ways of our people first."

Beth laughed. "No fear of that, Chief. He learns so fast anything put to him, it will not interfere. But my reasons are not purely because he is so bored. You can see that the white men are growing in number and like thunderclouds on a summer day, they build in strength by the minute. There will come a time when the people will need knowledge of the white man's ways, and reading their language will only be a help to the child, someday. It will make him wary and knowledgeable at the same time. But if you do not find it wise, I will not suggest it again."

"I see your logic, Shaman. And I trust your instincts. Perhaps now is the time to start teaching him what he will need when we are gone."

"You have taught him what he really needs. This will but give him a tool."

"And now I need your skills. I have had strange news of a man among a tribe near us, related by marriage in several ways, who is looking for a white woman. He is not a white, but his father was. I fear he seeks you."

Beth's heart stood still. It was what she had prayed for days, so hard she thought surely God was deaf. Someone sought a white woman, but not her. The chief awaited her response.

"I do not know who it is. My brother was a scout, but it cannot be him."

"I have not asked you about your people, Shaman, since you have become one of us. But now is, perhaps, the time. Is there anyone, besides your brother, who would be looking for you?"

She hesitated, wondering for a moment if her father would have set out, or decided she was already dead. "My father is a bluecoat, Grandfather, one who commands others. I do not know if he would search me out. He would do his duty, but I might not fall within his given command."

A slight frown creased the chief's ageless face. "What kind of father would not seek his daughter!" He hesitated. "Forgive me, I intrude. It is not my place to ask such a question. But I fear . . . "

"Yes, I know, my chief. You fear that someone will make trouble for the People, in trying to find me. Perhaps I should journey to this tribe with the half-blood who asks for a white woman. I will tell him I am not the one he seeks."

The decision was immediate. She hadn't really thought about it—it just seemed to be the correct thing to do. Be polite, but firm, and assure the man she was safe and did not want rescuing.

"No need for you to set forth in this weather, Shaman. I will summon the man here."

She nodded her assent. She had no idea who it could

be, her memories of her white life had grown so dim. She could see clearly her father and brother, and scenes from her childhood, but everything else was a gray mist. She wanted it that way.

Chapter Sixteen

It was the sort of winter Noble hated with a passion. Anything below freezing, and he felt subhuman. He and Rebecca spoke little during the long gray days, as the snows fell. He read aloud to her as she cooked and sewed, and she helped him in and out of the bed so he could sit by the fire, make water in the pot, and prop his leg on a stool. But at least it was starting to itch, and his hopes soared that the healing was almost complete.

"What you think, doc, can I sit a saddle any time soon?" he'd asked her casually one evening after they'd finished their allotted chapters in the Defoe.

Her red hair was straighter in the dry cold, and fell in long wisps into her eyes as she stitched a shirt for him. Shoving it out of her face with the back of a small-boned hand, she stared. "Trying to get rid of me, Noble? My company not good enough?" She tried to sound joking.

"Lord, no, Rebecca." He was horrified she would even jest about such a thing. "It's just that I could be of some help, and not such a burden to you. Why, you have to do everything—tend the horses, firewood, cooking . . . ''

"You're my patient, Noble McFarland. It's all right. I don't feel like you're a shirker. Remember, how I put all those little pieces of bone back in their proper places?"

"Well, not really." He laughed at his foggy memory.

"Just as well." She'd softened.

"I'd miss you." The words hung heavy in the air.

"I'd miss you too."

They stared across the short space between them, the unspoken question still there.

"I'll have to leave when I can, you know."

"Why? Where do you have to go? You still can't remember why you came here in the first place."

"But I will. And we both know it."

She turned her face from the light of the fire and held her forehead in her hands. He could see the struggle in her face, but she was a plain-speaking woman. He waited.

"Do you want me?"

"You know the answer to that." He reached for her hand and stroked it gently. "I've wanted you since I first saw you."

She hesitated, her eyes fearful, staring just beyond his shoulder. "I know."

The ache within him was more than he could stand.

Knotting his stomach, it gnawed at him like vultures. "Talk with me. Please."

"I don't know what to say." Still she wouldn't face him. He wanted more than anything to pull her head to his shoulder, stroke her hair, tell her he could marry her.

"Once my memory comes back, and I know where I stand."

"As far as a wife, you mean." Her voice was hard.

"Yes." The issue lay between them like a knife.

"What if it didn't matter to me if you were already married?" Now she stared into his eyes.

"But it would, Rebecca, and we both know it." He watched the shadows deepen within her eyes, and part of him longed for another answer than the one he'd get.

"Like a long, hard winter, it'll always be between us, won't it?" Pulling the rocker closer to him, she sat beside him, clutching one of his hands between her own.

He longed to pull her to him, to gently kiss her lips with his and feel the fire in her soul. "Yes. But that doesn't mean I don't love you. That will never change."

Startled, she started to pull away. "Who said anything about love?"

"That's what we've been talking about here, unless I've totally lost my senses. And I don't think a broken leg affects the brain, at least not just now. I love you.

I want to marry you. And if I'm free, I will, that is, if you'll have me.''

She laughed softly, the tension still in her eyes. ''That's the most backdoor proposal I've ever heard, and I've heard a few.''

He waited for an answer. ''Well? Yes or no?''

''I can't say for sure, Noble, and that's the honest truth. It's not that I don't want to say yes, it's just that with the not knowing and all, I think we'll have to say the best I can do is wait and see. For all I know, you may ride out of here and forget I ever existed.''

Holding the nape of her neck, he drew her down to his lips and gave her the kiss he'd been saving for weeks. Struggling slightly, she pushed at his chest with knotted fists, until he felt her fingers slacken and finally entwine themselves around his neck. He kissed her as he knew he'd never kissed anyone before, sealing their bargain with a promise of passion he could barely control. Gasping, she fought herself loose.

''Yes.'' Her eyes shone like silver conchos, her hair loose like tendrils of fire around her small face.

''I'll send you word as soon as I know. Then we'll get married, and take it from there.'' It wasn't a promise of a golden future—of that much he was sure, but somehow, he knew it wouldn't matter to her.

''Yes,'' was all she said to him again, and then her mouth sought out his.

Chapter Seventeen

The raid was planned well in advance. Since the death of Little Mountain, there had been no major chief over the People of Our Kind, and the councils had split beneath other leaders. Beth's tribe fell under the sway of Kicking Bird, who felt the People had to learn the white man's ways to survive.

Beth listened to the talk of war, as those who followed Big Bow prepared to raid into Texas and Mexico. Realizing that the farther south the tribe moved, the farther she would be from Fort Larned, she felt a slight moment of panic. Although she didn't expect rescue, or even need it, she longed to hear that Noble and her father were alive, and someday to tell them that she too was fine. But it was still too risky.

There was a captive Mexican who had been raised from childhood by the Kiowa in the band about to strike for Mexico. Beth had seen him at a distance; his build was stockier than most of the People. He was called Struck His Head Against a Tree. His reputation as a powerful warrior was well known. One day, he sought her out, asking entrance into the lodge she shared now with Grandfather and the boy.

None of the men related to Grandfather were present when he scratched. She assumed he had made a mistake, thinking Burning Bear was present.

"Enter," she answered, busy with beadwork on a pair of moccasins for the boy. She'd learned quickly that industry was a prized character trait for women, and had discovered that it gave her a sense of inner self-worth she'd never had before. Now, her hands were never idle, and what she didn't know, other women politely tried to teach her. Yet it was still acknowledged that her primary position was that of shaman, and that her healing work took precedence over menial tasks. What she did with her hands was for her own pleasure.

The brave loomed over her, waiting for her bid to sit. Startled, she wondered if he'd come to take her to someone who needed her prayers and art. She gestured for him to take an honored place.

Still wrapped in his buffalo robe, he solemnly sat cross-legged before her.

"Burning Bear is not here, my guest. I will be happy to tell him you have come to visit." She spoke slowly, carefully phrasing her words.

Struck His Head Against a Tree nodded. "I will speak with your grandfather later, if you permit, Shaman. But first, I must talk with you." He waited politely for her nod to continue.

"You know we raid in a few days' time. I have had a vision, and it concerns you. It must be told."

Putting aside the moccasins, Beth folded her hands politely. A vision was respected by one and all, and she knew it must be a serious matter for him to want to discuss it with her, a woman shaman. The older male shaman, after seeing the boy healed that night, had given his blessing to her for her curing ways. But still, she was surprised a respected warrior would come to her.

"In my vision, I was told that you have great power, mighty medicine. This is well known. I was also shown that my medicine, while strong, would become more powerful if we were to unite. If I return alive from this war party, I am to ask Burning Bear if he will accept a bride gift for you. But first, I must know your feelings."

She was stunned. The thought that a Kiowa brave would ask for her hand had never occurred to her. Her silence fell between them like a hot rock.

"I am more than honored, my words fail me. I had no knowledge that you might seek such an audience with my grandfather." She was buying time, trying to lessen the insult when she turned him down.

"In my vision, our sacred power was a wonder to all. Our sons will be inheritors of this strength, and do much good for our People." Struck His Head Against a Tree faced her calmly.

In a split second, she knew the full import of the vision. Kicking Bird's followers would eventually find a way to follow the peace road with the whites. Struck

His Head Against a Tree belonged to the followers of
White Bear's red-painted, fiercely independent ways.
If there was a uniting of their paths, she a shaman of
the peaceful side, he a famous fighter for the more
bellicose, there might be a way out of the dilemma.
The council had not yet chosen a principal leader. Was
there a way, she wondered, that such a match, a purely
political one, would help the Kiowa in the future?

"Forgive me for my unmaidenly ways, I beg of
you." She knew her behavior was not typical of a
maiden being asked to marry a famous warrior. But
then, she was the shaman. Struck His Head Against a
Tree was not seeking the typical bride. She realized
full well he knew the complete import of his propo-
sition.

"I have not considered marriage, but I see the wisdom of your vision. Please, give me time to seek my
own vision. I must know that our medicine will unite
with harmony, and not discord."

Struck His Head Against a Tree smiled slightly. She
sensed that she had avoided offending him, and was
pleased with herself.

"I am leaving in two suns' time. Will you have your
vision by then, Shaman?"

He was pointed, she had to give him that. It was
important to him, as to any warrior who saw a path he
must follow, to preserve his medicine, to know what
her answer might be. There was no passion to his

prompting, merely a request that she move the matter along.

"We will see, my friend, we will see. I will speak to no one of your vision, until I too can see clearly how it must be." She was giving him an out, should she refuse him. No one need ever know, even Grandfather.

Struck His Head Against a Tree bowed solemnly. He was strong, well muscled, respected, a young man in his prime. He had done her a great honor, and she knew it. Her white breeding should be shocked that she could even consider such a proposal. But the shaman side of her saw its wisdom.

It also meant she could never go home again.

As Struck His Head Against a Tree bowed out of her lodge, it hit her. What did it matter? If she ever saw her people again, they would all believe she had slept with every Kiowa man who wanted her. Her maidenhood was no protection from vicious gossip and the hard eyes of other white women who would wonder how she had had the audacity to survive such desecration. Her way had been sealed by the very act of living.

She decided to pray about the matter. It was the only way she knew she would get the answer she could live with. She sat silently and felt no need to direct her thoughts.

She saw Struck His Head Against a Tree before her, riding. He was painted for war. Then she knew he would not return from the raid. She didn't need to make a decision, it had been made for her. She wasn't aware of how much time had passed, until she sensed someone beside her.

"Grandfather," she said, nodding politely and opening her eyes. "I have had a vision."

"It has to do with your visitor?"

She should have known she couldn't hide it from him. The word would have been out almost immediately that she had been paid a call by a great warrior. Grandfather would know all about it.

"Yes, it does," she replied as she shook her head sorrowfully. "It is not good. Struck His Head Against a Tree does me great honor, but he will not live to come home."

Grandfather sat in his place of honor, sorrow etching his face deeper. "This saddens me, Granddaughter. He would have made a fine husband for you."

"Do not tell the vision, Grandfather. I would not have him mourned before his time."

She knew a death vision was rare among women. But her grandfather believed her. They stared into each other's eyes, sorrow in his, fear in hers. She didn't want such foreknowledge. And her grandfather knew it. She was shaman enough, without the sight of death to come. It was a burden she couldn't share with anyone.

Chapter Eighteen

The ache in Noble's muscles felt good. He'd walked the length of the front porch twenty times, sucking in the cold air and feeling his blood pound through his legs for the first time in weeks. It was still blasted cold, but he reveled in it. He was on his feet, with no help from Rebecca.

Slamming back into the cabin, he ached for Rebecca. Her calm face was cut with lines across her forehead and at the corner of her mouth. But she gave him a brief smile, glancing up from her piecing. The squares of old cloth littered her lap as she fashioned a quilt for him to take when he rode out. So far she'd kept quiet about his plans, although he knew she burned with questions he couldn't answer.

"Feels good. Hurts like it's supposed to."

"Means the muscles are limbering up. I'll give you a rub."

"No need." He jerked off her husband's old boots. They were at least two sizes too large for him, but they didn't cut at the top into his leg. He was afraid of her hands, afraid he'd never be able to leave her warm touch.

''Frank'll be over in a few days to check up on you, you might try askin' him if they can spare you some extra tack. Might be worn out, but you've got time to do some mending.''

It was upon him at last. His leg was no reason to stay any longer. He had to tell her.

''Got all I need now. Horse, saddle, bridle, bit. You've packed me enough jerky and hardtack to last till next Christmas. It's time I headed out, Rebecca.''

Her needle stopped in midair. ''Which way you heading?''

''Guess I'll aim for an Army post. Stay on the road. Maybe someone'll recognize me.''

''What if you're a wanted man?'' She stared at him eye to eye.

''Guess anything's possible. If I pick up a rope, I'll make sure you get the message.''

''Don't make promises you may not be able to keep, Noble.'' Disgusted, she jerked to her feet, scattering the scraps of wool and cotton.

He had no idea she feared for his life so intensely. So far, he felt only her shame at loving a man who was possibly married.

''I'm not wanted. Why would I have been in the saloon, asking to be found, the night I got shot? Doesn't make sense, Rebecca. No, truth is, I've got to find her. The woman with the blond hair. I won't be free until I do.''

''I know.'' Crouching, she stuffed the scraps into a

basket. "I'll finish the quilt while you're gone. Take the red blanket off your bed. Bring it back when you come, it's my best one."

Lord, how he wanted to stay. Was it worth it, this leave-taking? He might never again see the curls at the nape of her neck when she swept her braid to one side. But he'd never be able to tell her about the last dream, the one in which he saw the woman surrounded by dead soldiers, struggling in the arms of a Kiowa brave as he hauled her over the withers of his horse. The vision had left him sweaty, jerking upright in bed, knowing he had to ride out as soon as he could bear his own weight.

Slamming at her once-risen bread, Rebecca turned her back to him at the worktable. He sensed her need to be alone. But more than anything, he wanted to hold her in his arms for the few hours they had left, to memorize every bone in her body as she hugged him. Her back bent to the task at hand. He touched her waist.

"Don't," she snapped. "Just don't."

"But . . . " He couldn't think of an answer. "She's not my wife. I'd feel something whenever I see her face, something like I feel for you. I don't. I sense love, but it's not that kind of love."

"Just talk, Noble. You can't even remember her full name. I won't be letting myself love you until you're free of her. And if you can't be free, then I'll do just fine on my own. Been alone a long time now, it's my way.''

He retreated, slipping in his socks on the throw rug. Off balance, he clutched at the table. Sensing his predicament, Rebecca snaked an arm around his waist.

''Don't you go messing up my mend, Noble McFarland.'' She left her arm around his waist.

''Nothing I'd like more. Keep me here with you.'' He nuzzled her hair. He meant it. Then his gut twisted with the dream of the blonde and the Kiowa.

''Then maybe you'd better ride now.'' Once again, she turned from him, smashing a fist into her dough.

Twirling her to face him, he gave her a last kiss. It meant more than a kiss, and they both knew it. With only the willpower born of a desperate desire to marry her, he slid away, panting.

''I'll go now.''

Jerking on his worn jacket, Noble stomped into his boots. Every part of him screamed he was being a fool. Grabbing the saddlebags Rebecca had been filling with provisions, he lunged for the door.

''Wait,'' she called him back, her voice small. ''Don't forget the blanket.''

He couldn't look her in the eyes as she thrust it at him. Twisting it over his shoulder, he lunged through the cold to the barn. The horse wouldn't be happy pulling out in early afternoon. It would be dark before long. He'd aim for Frank's ranch, spend the night, then find the road in the morning.

One more night with Rebecca so near, yet so far, was more than he could stand. Maybe he was a widower. If he was lucky.

Chapter Nineteen

The guard had been set on the horses. Night rose with the moon as an owl screeched. Johnny hunkered down, scratching a hole for his shoulder, the dirt feeling cool and moist under his fingers. Excitement had left him drained, and he wanted sleep more than anything. He was grateful it wasn't his job to guard the herd. They had celebrated into the night, confident in their prowess and the good favor of the gods.

The moon was high, an orange dollop bright enough to set the grass on fire. Johnny fretted, unable to sleep despite the bone-weariness that pinned him down. Then he heard it. A whistle that didn't belong, a call from a coyote he hadn't heard in the hours he'd spent ruminating about the day's plunder. Gently, he levered the rifle, the click louder than a man crunching dry twigs.

Fast Cloud was instantly beside him.

"Listen," Johnny hissed.

Fast Cloud exhaled slowly, every muscle tense. "Soldiers?" he muttered into Johnny's ear.

Once again, the coyote called, only from another direction.

"No," Johnny mouthed. They both knew no white man could call like a coyote.

Fast Cloud crept up to a sleeping man and pressed his palm to his mouth as he shook him. One by one, they roused the others, sliding in the moonlight as carefully as possible. The burble of the creek beside their camp masked the little noise they made as they slid into the herd, each man armed.

Johnny locked his fingers in the first mane he could grab, and hoisted himself up. Even bareback with no reins, he'd have a better chance. Fast Cloud had circled out to warn the guards, when they hit.

They slammed in from the east, their shrieks ripping through the night like lost souls. Johnny crouched low on the neck of his horse, waiting to see a man before he aimed. He didn't want to nick any of the herd by accident. The guards returned the cry, whooping the signal to attack as more of the marauders crashed into the trap. Johnny flipped up as a lone man on a big dark horse thundered down upon him.

"Yieah!" he chortled as he drove his lance into the man's thigh. The glancing blow knocked his enemy to the ground, and Johnny leaped to finish the job. Throwing himself to one side, the warrior locked Johnny with a grip that surprised him. It had been much too long since he'd fought hand to hand, Johnny realized as an iron fist locked onto his throat. Jabbing the heel of his palm into a chin, Johnny added a knee to the groin.

There was a satisfying "oomph," and the enemy

twisted into a knot under Johnny. Unleashed from the death grip on his neck, Johnny rolled off, scrabbling in the dirt for his lance. He would kill the man and be done with it. Hooves flailed around him as the herd swirled around fighting men. Johnny could no longer tell who was enemy and who was Comanche.

His fingers finally found the wooden shaft. Hoisting it, he knew he was a target, but the blood lust pounded through him. He didn't care, he would kill this thief, this belly-crawler who would steal from him, when the moon ducked out from the cloud that had smothered it for a moment.

Grimacing in the dirt was no enemy. Kiowa and Comanche had often fought and raided together.

"Why do you steal from brothers?" Johnny snarled in Kiowa.

Startled, the man uncorked slightly to stare into Johnny's face. Tossing his lance to the ground, Johnny hoisted the man to his feet.

"You are of the Kiowa?" he spit into the man's ear.

"Yes," gasped the wounded warrior. "Who are you?"

"We are the People, Comanche. You steal from allies."

"We thought you were Navajo. . . . " The man groaned. "So many horses, we saw the tracks. . . . "

Johnny sent him sliding down again, and twirling, reached for the first horse near him. Vaulting onto its back, he screamed for his compatriots.

"We fight the Kiowa!" Shouting into the night, he plunged into the foray, knowing that the instinct to survive would dull many ears. Surely, he hoped, some of them had realized by now that they fought their allies, and hoped that the number of deaths would be few. Otherwise, they would have to pay most of the herd to compensate the families of friends.

"Fast Cloud!" He shouted above the din of screaming horses. A familiar figure loomed beside him, breathless, on foot.

"Kiowa!" he screamed. Fast Cloud stood rooted to the spot.

Quickly Johnny heeled the horse to circle the camp, shouting the warning. In Kiowa, he sang out the name of his tribe, warning they were friend, not foe.

Slowly the fighting wound down, as blood lust died with knowledge that they fought ancient compatriots. The moon sailed across the night, and scattered horses began to nuzzle the ground for a calming bit of grass. Panting men lay strewn about the camp, the smell of blood thick with the aroma of horseflesh.

Johnny waited for his war chief. His job was done— he'd stopped a massacre of an ancient ally, which would have brought much bad medicine to his tribe. Fast Cloud sought him out, giving him a cuff to the shoulder.

"Twice you bring honor to us, old friend," Fast Cloud muttered as he sank to his haunches beside Johnny. "This was not good, tonight, but it would have brought us lasting shame to be robbed in the night like women!''

The night guards were rounding up the scattered herd as others roused a fire, warming the camp and giving them light. Johnny counted ten Kiowa he could see. Few were wounded; most of the Comanche stood around sullenly, their excitement of a few moments earlier stifled by the knowledge they were lusting to kill an ally.

''Come, sit,'' called the war chief, rising. Slowly a few men crumpled, too wounded or tired to do anything else. It had been a close call, too close. Johnny and Fast Cloud edged to the fire.

''We would smoke the pipe, and be done with this bad business, but our lodges are far from here. Why do you attack a friend?''

A tall Kiowa, more muscular than most, rose. ''We fought the Navajo, we believed. Had we known you were old friends, we would never have brought such shame upon ourselves. We will make a visit on your lodges and bring offerings of peace.''

Johnny smiled to himself. Normally, there would have been a long and lengthy powwow to decide the outcome of the breach of etiquette, but both raid chiefs realized they'd do better by getting down to the business at hand. Johnny's people had almost been taken unawares. Likewise, the Comanche had made an error that might have meant war. It would not do to have such mistakes generally well known.

The Comanche war chief counted his men. "We are all alive. There is no blood spilled that cannot be healed. We will forget tonight, except to remember that Comanche and Kiowa have been friends for many winters."

It was a generous gesture. Johnny and Fast Cloud raised eyebrows to each other, knowing it meant they'd ride on, instead of returning home. The wounded who needed more tending would be sent back, but there was more glory to come. Johnny thrilled in the knowledge.

Then it struck him. These were the people who had taken Beth. Would this band know about her? There was almost no way they wouldn't, if she were alive.

With a sickening knot in his stomach, Johnny felt himself drifting back into the white part of himself. He'd made a promise, and he would have to keep it. Even if it meant leaving his tribe.

The Comanche chief continued. "Come, sleep what is left to us beside our fires. We will talk more when the sun rises."

Johnny edged his way toward the big Kiowa, the one who looked more Mexican than of the People. He saluted, man to man, warrior to warrior. The Kiowa returned the gesture, his face impassive.

"I am called Little Fox by my people," Johnny began in Kiowa.

"How do you know my tongue?" the warrior answered warily. "You do not use sign."

"I was raised many places. The Kiowa were some of my boyhood friends."

The other nodded. It wasn't unusual for children to be sent to spend time with allied tribes, learning their languages and ways. The horses had settled, a few nickers here and there breaking the settling noises of the night. Veins that had been pounding with blood lust not twenty minutes earlier were slowly settling into rest. Sleep was still far away.

"You wish something of me?" The Kiowa hunkered down on his haunches, his face wary.

The man was smart, Johnny realized as he sank down beside him. "Only to talk. I have heard of a white woman among your people, and wish to know if you have knowledge of her. Forgive my bluntness, but she is related to me in a fashion. I would like to find her, and you are the first Kiowa I have seen in many moons."

The other grunted. "My name is Struck His Head Against A Tree. Is this woman a slave?"

Johnny shrugged. "I have no way of knowing. If so, then I will pay ransom for her. She is sister to my blood brother."

Struck His Head Against a Tree snorted. "You, a Comanche, blood brother to the white eyes?"

"To one. My mother's people are the Comanche, my father rode the white soldier's road." Johnny could sense the other man tensing. "I chose my mother's people. But I have promised my blood brother I would ask for his sister, if ever I could.''

The request hung between them like a threat. Johnny consciously relaxed, stretching out as though seeking sleep. His folded hands belied his tension.

''We have a white woman who dwells within our tents,'' snapped Struck His Head Against a Tree. ''She is the granddaughter of one of our oldest and wisest chiefs. We have treated her well, and she chooses a life among the People.'' The words cracked with emotion. Johnny rolled over to search the face of the warrior in the waning firelight.

''Is this woman's white name Beth?'' It could only be her, he prayed.

''I do not know,'' snarled Struck His Head Against a Tree. ''To me—to us—she is Mythmaker. She has great powers to heal. She is one of us.'' Tossing his blanket over his shoulder, the Kiowa slumped back as though to sleep.

Johnny itched with excitement. It could only be Beth; the fighter hadn't mentioned any other white captives. Beth would have survived, and even more, made herself one of them, indispensable. Johnny ached to press the man for even more, for a conduct to his village that very night, to see if it was Beth.

But these were raiding parties, both of them. The Kiowa were bound for the Navajo, they rode for more horses and coups. It would take awhile, but he would find the tribe that held Beth.

"Thank you, my friend," whispered Johnny, knowing when to leave it alone. "I will someday come and visit your tribe, and wish my sister well."

Struck His Head Against a Tree grunted again. "Then ask for her at my lodge, for she will be my wife."

Johnny had to bite his lip. Beth would never come home to Noble and her father now.

Chapter Twenty

Beth stroked the soft fur moccasins against the boy's sleeping face. "Awake, little one. Time for our lesson."

He shoved at the fur, curling into a tighter ball. "Ummph."

Beth laughed. The winter had done nothing to improve his humor, and there was little she could do to amuse him, as he yearned to romp and hunt with boundless energy.

"Your grandfather is coming today to see your progress. You don't want to disappoint him, do you?"

That got him. Instantly awake, he rubbed his eyes and began ambling toward the food pot. "I won't disappoint him, will I, Mythmaker?"

"Of course not. You've learned well."

She'd used dried berries for the ink concoction and trimmed some old feathers for pens. The hard part had been finding a surface similar to parchment, and she'd finally hit on her own version of paper by soaking old skins and drying them too close to the fire. There was no hope of finding chalk and a slate, which would have made it easier for the boy. But his small, pudgy fingers

132

had adjusted fairly well to the homemade quills, and his alphabet was credible.

Patting a spot beside her, she settled him down after his morning gulp of breakfast. "Now, little one, you make the next figure like this." She shifted his hand on the quill, slowly tracing a large *m*.

"This is how you say this letter." She exaggerated the shape of her mouth, hopeful he would get it correct the first time. He'd been so eager to learn, and so quick, that she didn't want him to become discouraged.

He pronounced the *m* easily, laughing at the shape of her mouth as she mimicked him.

"Bravo!"

"What does that mean?" He was swift to question everything she said during the lessons.

"Only that you have done well. I think I will give you one more letter for today, and that will be all for your practice."

"Pshaw. I can do more."

"I know, but you must show Grandfather everything you have learned. Will you practice this morning, without me? I must do something for a short while, and you need only practice while I am gone. Then we can go and visit Grandfather and show him your work."

"Where are you going without me?" he wailed like a lost lamb. She felt a twinge of guilt, knowing how much he hated being cooped up.

"Just to see someone. I will tell you later all about it." It was time she explained more to him of who she really was. She might have to leave some day, and it would be harder for each moment she didn't prepare him. At the thought of leaving the tribe, her hands began to shake. Just yesterday she had helped at a difficult birth, and only her long, thin fingers had been able to turn the baby so it could be born. Her healing powers seemed to grow each day she was with the tribe, and never in her life had she felt so wanted and useful.

"Are you really coming back?"

Pulling his tiny body to hers, Beth smoothed the hair from his forehead. "Of course. I am your shaman."

"Grandfather says a shaman's spirit never leaves a tribe, once it has come, and that even if you were stolen from us, you would see to it that your spirit remains."

"Your grandfather is very wise." The child's words told her how much the chief feared her going. "But this morning I am only going for a visit, and will return. So practice!"

Tossing the buffalo robe over her head, she left the child hunched over his lesson. It was a meeting she would rather have avoided, but the chief had sent a special messenger to bring the Comanche to her. She knew it had been at her request, but still she trembled at what she might hear.

The sun cracked through the winter gray of the sky, spreading a false warmth through her. For the sake of the tribe, they needed to know who sought her, and how much of a threat traveled with her seeker.

Scratching on the door to the tepee of the chief's respected brother-in-law, she waited for her signal to enter. Heart thumping like a trapped fawn's, she pulled the robe closer to her face, hoping to hide her identity until she could make out the features of her searcher.

"Enter." She ducked in, keeping her head low until her eyes adjusted to the dimness.

"Daughter," the chief spoke first, "this man is Little Fox, of our cousins, the Comanche. He has lived many years among the white eyes, and says he has sought you for your brother's sake. Do you know him?"

"My God," she moaned in English. "Johnny."

He saluted her with the sign of respect reserved for a shaman. "Shaman," he whispered in Kiowa, "my cousins told me of you, and I feared to hope it was truly you."

Knowing it was poor manners to use English, she dropped the robe and knelt in the small circle of men.

"Grandfather, this is my brother's blood brother. We grew up together, as children. He is well known to me."

The tension in the room became taut as an overstrung bow. She knew the chief had hoped she'd deny any knowledge of this man.

"So, cousin," the chief said to jump into the silence that followed, "why do you seek the sister of your blood brother? Have you heard that she has been mistreated among us? Fed like a dog?'' Disdain and slighted pride dripped from every word.

Quick to assuage the chief, Johnny was all humility. ''Not at all, Chief. It is simple, really. I came home, and heard talk of the white shaman from your warriors. I merely wondered, since the sister of my blood brother had been missing since last summer, if it could be she. I meant no harm, only the joy of seeing an old friend again.''

Beth followed the speech carefully, knowing it was rehearsed. But would the chief know?

''I am honored by Little Fox's visit. It has been many moons since we were children together. Would he care to come to my tepee, and talk of the old days? Your grandson is eager to show off his new knowledge to you, my grandfather.''

She felt the tension draining slowly from the group around the fire. Her calm and his casualness had allayed some of the worst fears that the white eyes were marching toward them even as they spoke. But not quite all of the tension had dissipated.

The chief's brother-in-law cut into the congeniality. ''Do the white eyes search for our shaman now, Little Fox?''

Johnny looked deeply into her eyes. ''They do not, my brother. At least, when I last saw the father of your shaman, he was not searching for her. That was at least eight moons ago. It has been long since I saw her brother. They believe her to be dead, I heard.''

Part of Beth crumpled. Not even Noble had hoped she'd survive. It was what she'd have expected, but not what she wanted to hear.

"Good," she found herself chanting softly. "Good. Then I am free to remain with my people without fear of the white eyes."

Johnny's hard, dark eyes bore into hers. "The choice is yours, my brother's sister. It has always been yours."

She rose to go. "Please come visit my tepee when you are free. Chief, shall I send your grandson to you now, or wait for you to call him?"

"I will come to him now, Daughter. Little Fox has promised to stay awhile, and you two have many memories to relive. It may as well be now in the comfort of my lodge."

She silently applauded his tact. He knew that if there was more to Johnny's story, she'd tell him.

"Thank you for your hospitality," she responded formally as the two men left the tepee. Turning to Johnny, she found her arms open to him, and they hugged in silence for many minutes.

"So, a shaman? You must have mighty medicine, Beth." Johnny spoke in English, and Beth was startled.

"It just happened. I have found a place for myself here. And respect." It was taking effort to speak her own tongue, it had been so long.

"Do you want to know the truth? About what happened after the wagon was found?"

Beth hesitated. "I'm not sure. I can't lie to the chief, and he will want to know everything we talk about. Yet I suppose I must know the truth someday. I'm just not sure now is the time."

Johnny waited. Beth had changed from a pretty young girl into a woman with lines of wisdom at the edges of her eyes. He'd expected to find her half dead, a slave at best. Yet she exuded an aura of contentment and peace that belied the worst of Noble's fears.

"I'll do as you wish. It is your life, my friend."

Beth let out a high-pitched and almost girlish laugh. "Do you know that is a very Comanche way of thinking? You have not become so white after all, Johnny."

"Maybe not. It was hard to go back to the tribe, but it was the only way."

She knew what he was going to say if he continued. "To find me."

"Yes. More. Find myself." Johnny laid a twig on the small warm fire in the middle of the tepee. "I promised Noble I'd meet him in one month's time from now. We'd decide where to take it from there."

"The search for me." She pictured Noble freezing to death on the plains, hunting for clues of her whereabouts.

"Why didn't he give up, since I assume my father did?"

"He didn't." Johnny spoke gently. "He sent Noble. Noble and I had a better chance of making sure you stayed alive, if you still were, than a herd of bluecoats thundering after some renegades. Your father also knew he'd never be able to stay out as long as we would, that the Army doesn't understand taking its troops on a personal trip to find one's own daughter.''

It had been easier to imagine that they all thought her dead, and their grieving was almost over. ''I should have been—dead that is—but for you. I remembered stories you told us, when we were children, about how to survive. I used them, Johnny. And for that I have to thank you for my life.''

Johnny took one of her tanned hands between his. ''And after that? What happened to make you become one of us—survival?''

She smiled into his eyes, seeing a new Johnny she'd never known before. A man. A man who cared for her as much as her own family. It had not escaped her that he'd referred to her tribe as ''us,'' and not ''them.''

''No, much more than that. A child. Magpie. It's a long story. Come and meet him.''

Johnny followed her through the deep snow, the sun glistening on its softness for the first time in days, and sensed that Beth had made her decision long before he'd come. There was no doubt in his mind, and now he had to think of what he was going to tell Noble. A lie, in many ways, would be kinder than the truth. Noble was still too white in his thinking to understand Beth wanting to stay with the tribe. He would think that Johnny was hiding the real truth, and still search for his sister. And that would be a disaster for them all.

"Is he yours? The boy?" Johnny knew it was not possible, but it would explain much.

"Oh, no!" Beth laughed. "Although you would think so. His mother's dead, his father killed by Navajo. No, he's my adopted son, although nothing formal." Suddenly, she realized what he'd thought.

"No," she added gently. "I don't feel too sullied to go home. Nothing like that." She reached for his hand. "Nothing so silly. Although I know what people would think, how it would be. At the post, that is."

He noticed she hadn't said "at home." They were closer now than they'd been throughout their entire childhood.

"Have you taken a husband, Shaman?"

Startled, she hesitated. "No. A brave warrior asked, but he was killed in battle."

"Will you marry, if you stay?"

"I don't know." She avoided his glance. "My destiny is still unclear to me."

She led the way to the tepee that held her boy and her grandfather. Johnny spoke to her from then on only in Kiowa.

Chapter Twenty-one

Noble cringed with every jarring trot of the old gelding. The leg throbbed, his side still ached, and he wished like the devil he was back with Rebecca. Frank had been thrilled, in fact, too thrilled to see him on horseback, and heading away from Rebecca's place. Envy chewed at Noble's guts, along with the pain of long-unused muscles. Frank would find other reasons for visiting the young widow, now that Noble was gone. The cold seeped into Noble's blood, but he didn't know which was more chilling, the weather or the thought of Frank alone with Rebecca.

He'd found few houses at which to put up for the night. The trail so far had been sodden with wet snow, and he thought he'd never get dry again. Too many soft nights in Rebecca's spare bed, he chided himself. He hadn't been so spoiled when he'd first found himself awakened to her redheaded visage. Instinctively, he shied away from trying to seek any memories. It was a simple fact that he'd been tough as nails before the broken leg and the shooting, but more than that, he'd still been unable to admit his true feelings to himself. Perhaps he didn't want to know more.

The Arkansas Road to Fort Larned was getting wider, more visible. Noble hunkered down and pushed the horse with his heels. If he was going to get there before night, he'd have to suffer with more than a trot. The gelding broke into a small canter, twisting Noble in the saddle with his swinging gait. He cursed.

The sun was lowering, winter-early, into the edge of the sky when Noble caught a first glimpse of the square configuration of the fort. Lantern lights glimmered faintly from windows as the post settled in for a cold night. Noble sawed on the gelding's mouth, uncertain of his future. If he were wanted for some crime, there'd be a stockade waiting. But if not, if he were truly just another drifter on the plains, he'd have to keep riding. But somehow the symmetry of the post, its neat, square buildings and barracks, seemed familiar to him.

The trumpet carried as far as Noble while the huge garrison flag was lowered from its one-hundred-foot pole for the night. The echo of the instrument's last note carried like a thread in the wind, and Noble curled his cold toes in Rebecca's husband's boots. The music had caught him unawares, and he knew it was a sound he'd heard too often for it to be just a chance of a memory.

Spurring the gelding, Noble raced for the post, clattering past the blockade as though all the Indian nations were on his tail. If there was something to find at Fort Larned, he'd find it now.

The clatter of his horse sent troopers scurrying.

"Ho, there!" shouted a sergeant, racing from the shops building, blocking Noble's charge for the parade ground.

Reining in, Noble spit out the breath he'd been saving, hoping a face would appear out of the last of twilight and call him by name. The sergeant stared at Noble, his gloved hands sawing on the horse's reins as the gelding frisked with the raking he'd taken from Noble's spurs.

"Whoa, there, son, who's on your tail? Cheyenne? What's the all-fire hurry here, boy?" The trooper hauled the horse to a stand, as men ran with rifles to surround Noble.

"What's the problem, son?" the sergeant reiterated.

"Nothin'," Noble spit out, still gasping from the pain of the mad charge for the post. "Take a good look at me, Sergeant, you know my face?" The building directly in front of him, a house across the parade grounds, seemed too familiar.

The shadows were almost complete. Noble swung down, his bad leg crumpling from his weight. Slinging an arm under him, a trooper saved him from hitting dirt.

"Come on in, son, where we can get a better look. Supposed to know you, am I?" The sergeant flipped an order, and Noble's gelding was led away. The trooper keeping Noble on his feet helped him toward a barracks to the right of the parade ground. Noble sensed this was what he'd been looking for. If a blond woman came from the door of one of the quarters, he'd have only expected it.

The barracks were cold, lit by a few iron-bellied stoves around the sides. The trooper slung Noble on a cot. Shoving back his hat, Noble shrugged out of Rebecca's husband's old buffalo coat. The soldiers stared at him.

"Been a long time, son," the sergeant admitted. "Just about given you up for good. Don't look like yourself—mighty scrawny."

Noble's heart pounded like a hammer on a horseshoe.

"You know me, Sergeant, you sure about that?" His voice sounded rusty and dry.

"Pete's sake, Noble, your father's been gnawing knuckles, no word from you. Becker, get your tail over to the commandant's quarters. Tell him his son's here."

Noble sank back into the cot, fighting for breath. It was coming back, floodtides of memories, scenes from his childhood, his sister by his side, his mother, knowing she was dead. It was almost too much. Clutching the edges of the scratchy wool blanket covering the cot, he forced himself upright.

"My father, where?"

"On his way, boy. I'd take you over to him, but you look plumb worn out. What's the matter, Noble?

You act like you ain't never seen none of us afore.'' The grizzled old soldier patted Noble's shoulder.

''My father's Colonel McFarland, he's stationed here, and I'm a scout for the Army.''

''Right, sure you are. Now what's all this, you're acting like you've never set eyes on any of us afore, and here you've been scouting with us awhile now.''

Noble fought back the tears. The door burst open, and a tall, imposing man, shirt opened at the neck under the uniform coat, swirled down on him.

''Noble, son, what word? Did you find her? Alive?''

Noble searched the blue eyes that stared into his own dark ones, and knew he'd seen those same eyes in his dreams.

''Beth, you mean Beth, sir?''

He was home.

Chapter Twenty-two

Noble restitched the chin strap, savagely jabbing the leather strip with the awl. Twisting the headpiece from side to side, he searched anxiously for other mends to be made. There were none. It filled him with a sense of desolation, like the long gray winter stretching endlessly across the prairie. He had to ride again. Stomping across the parade ground, he steeled himself before the new sandstone commanding officer's quarters.

Clattering into the hallway, Noble's spurs rang out in the early morning.

"Sir," he shouted, "I'll be going now."

His father hunkered through the door to the parlor, his uniform precisely buttoned, insignia gleaming, boots black as Noble's mood.

"I see." The colonel squinted at him. "Provisions enough? Extras you'll need?"

The ache in the colonel's eyes matched Noble's. If he'd been Comanche, the colonel would have cut off a finger and bled from self-inflicted wounds, his despair for Beth was so palpable.

"Nothing else, sir. Tacked up, be riding out. Came

to say . . ." Noble almost said "farewell," but it was too much the way Beth would have said good-bye.

"Came to say you're heading out. Yes." His father flicked a palm to his forehead, a semisalute for a nonsoldier.

There hadn't been much said, the two of them existing in an uneasy silence in the small officer's house. Beth's room downstairs was shut, the closed door unbreachable.

"If she's dead, I won't be back," Noble finally blurted out. "Get word back to you, somehow."

"If I don't hear?" The colonel was almost hesitant, Noble's long absence hanging between them like a misfire.

"You'll know I'm dead too." Noble stared into the colonel's deep blue eyes.

There was nothing more to say. Twisting away, the colonel clutched his hands at the small of his back, fingers knotted like old leather. "Keep safe, son. Don't let 'em get you again."

"I'll try, sir." He knew his father hadn't meant it as a criticism. For the first time, he understood the depth of his father's love for both of his children, and marveled at it. It had simply been easier for the colonel to show Beth he loved her. Between fathers and sons, there would always be a wall hiding the strength of their affection. If he and Rebecca had children, would he be as loving a father?

Slamming onto the portico, Noble jammed his hands

into his gloves. There was nothing more to say. He'd given his word to his father, and he would keep it.

Dawn was a pale yellow streak as Noble mounted. Troopers scurried from the mess, the day just starting for them. Noble sawed on the reins, his horse eager to keep moving in the late winter cold. It might be the last time he'd see Fort Larned, his father, and the troopers he'd scouted with since he'd come to manhood.

Rebecca's face was before him. Beth was dead; there was no way she could have survived this long. But he'd do what he had to do, he'd hunt for her bones until he'd found every one. Johnny had to be gone also, or he'd have gotten word back to the fort. Their split paths had led to disaster for them both.

Suddenly, the trumpet shot through the dawn like cannon fire, shaking Noble from his depression. Noble's horse skittered, his hooves skidding on a patch of ice. The alarm raked through the post, troopers running pell-mell for arms. *Indians.*

Noble threw himself from the saddle, unscabbarding his rifle. This was the wrong time of year for raids. Racing for the edge of the barracks, Noble pulled his spyglass from his pocket. Scanning the old riverbed, the Oxbow, he relaxed when he saw only a lone figure.

There was no war paint on the brave, and his hair was unfeathered. A warrior's lance, white rag flapping in the morning breeze, waved back and forth. Dropping his glass, Noble raced for the sergeant.

"Peace flag, Sarge." The sergeant stared at Noble as though he'd chewed locoweed.

The brave's big bay pawed, and the Indian pushed him on. Noble passed his spyglass to the colonel, who'd come running as the trumpet sounded the alert. The Indian entered between the blockade and the shops building, heading straight for the heart of the parade ground.

"Expecting any peace commission?" Noble watched his father stare at the Indian. An uneasy quiet grew by the second, an anxious anticipation building like the last days of winter before a spring storm.

The colonel gestured for Noble to hand him his reins. Swinging into the saddle like a younger man, he tossed the glass to Noble.

"Follow me, scout. Think you might know this one."

Perplexed, Noble shouldered his rifle, butt cradled in his palm. The cold bit into his cheeks, and wet snow worked its way into the soles of his boots. He didn't want to know who was out there. The warrior halted at the advance of the colonel.

He was Comanche, Noble finally realized. The sun broke through the low-lying clouds, streaking the man in a swatch of light. Noble felt the ground swell under his feet.

Johnny. The Comanche was Johnny. Whooping Johnny's name, Noble edged ahead of the colonel. His father reined in, allowing Noble the first step.

Noble stared. He'd just given up his friend for dead. But why the Indian garb, the parlay gestures? Why didn't he come riding into the post like a scout?

Johnny dropped the lance, point down, tossing a leg over the withers as he slid to the ground. Noble rooted ten feet away, scouring Johnny's face for the old signs of camaraderie. The man across from him, hair loose about his face, a steely cast to his eyes, was a stranger.

Noble rumbled his throat, his lungs searching for air.

"Thought you were dead," he finally blurted out.

"Why?" There was a hint of a smile in Johnny's eyes. "Said I'd get word back, this winter."

"It's almost spring. Just about to set out again, myself." Noble was acutely aware every eye behind him was riveted on his back. The tension between him and Johnny strung out like a gut about to split.

"No need. She's alive. Found her."

Noble's bad leg buckled, pitching him into the slushy snow. Leaping to his side, Johnny steadied him.

"Alive? Where?" The lump in Noble's throat rebubbled.

"We'll talk." Hoisting Noble to his feet, Johnny stared into Noble's face. "Answers aren't easy," he whispered. "Your father won't want to hear this."

Limping beside Johnny, Noble's body worked by itself. His mind raced ahead, tossing out questions. The colonel sat rock-solid, unblinking as he threw a nod at Johnny. Noble straightened, forcing the leg to work. The troopers parted as the two of them trudged through the muddy snow bordering the parade ground. A buzz of whispers closed ranks behind them. The colonel watched them from the center of the parade ground.

Oblivious to his father, Noble led the way to his quarters. Johnny dropped the bay's reins, hoisting his lance against the edge of the porch. Blind to everyone and everything, Noble shoved the front door, mildly surprised as it slammed into the interior wall.

Johnny gently pushed it shut behind them. "Didn't expect to find you. Thought I'd have to tell the colonel."

"You will. Eventually." Noble rubbed his aching leg, avoiding Johnny's eyes. The news had to be bad, and he wasn't sure he wanted to hear it.

Johnny hesitated. "You need to sit. What's wrong with the leg?"

Noble nodded, inching his way to his father's horsehair settee, thinking that Beth would have been intrigued to see Johnny decked out in Comanche duds. "Got shot, my danged horse broke the leg at the same time. Took a crack to the head. Just got back, myself. Thought you were a goner, for sure. No sign or word from you." He wanted to ask about the Indian getup, but Beth was more important at the moment.

"Took awhile to find her. Guess you figured that out." Johnny's face flitted again with a ghostly smile.

"She didn't want me to tell you. 'Bout where she is. What she is."

"That bad?" Noble's insides turned to gruel.

"Depends on how you see it. White eyes think she's lost for good, I suppose. She feels found."

"Cut the palaver, Johnny, for God's sake! Tell me the worst, before my father marches in here! If we have to, we'll tell him she's dead!"

"That's what she wanted. For me to tell you she'd died. But the truth is, she's a woman of power with the Kiowa, a shaman. She has to live with the truth."

Noble stared. "Shaman? A medicine woman?"

"More than that. She's a healer. True healer. Adopted granddaughter to one of the great old men. Her visions are true."

Noble remembered enough of the tales of strong shamans that Johnny had taught him. "A woman, a shaman?" he puzzled aloud.

"Yeah, a woman." Johnny was almost mocking. "She says she'd never be so respected here. She'd always be just a woman."

Noble pulled at his jacket. "For Pete's sake, Johnny, you telling me she doesn't want to come back? She's staying there because she wants to?"

Johnny propped himself against the wall by the door, so Noble had to twist to see his face. "She said you'd never understand, better to let you think she's dead. Told her you'd find her bones, keep going till you did. Finally talked her into letting me tell you the truth. But don't go thinking you'll find her. She'll only come back if she decides it's right. Now, she's wanted, needed. Teaching the Kiowa children letters, reading. Never seen Beth like this—she's grown into her new name.''

Noble hesitated. ''What's that?''

''Mythmaker. She's the maker of legends. She'll lead the Kiowa into greatness, her people say.''

''Her own, I suppose.'' Noble's sarcasm was tinged with bitterness. Johnny even smelled Comanche. His stomach rolling, Noble stared at his hands. His old friend had to be lying. The whole story was too fantastic to be true. Beth, who hated to leave her room with an unmade bed, sleeping on the ground and eating out of a pot of dog stew? He laughed out loud, its harshness sinking into the stillness between them.

''Maybe.'' Johnny unrolled himself. ''Leave her alone, Johnny. Tell your father what you want, but don't try to find her. She'll come back if she thinks the time is right, and only then. Save yourself some grief.''

''Grief! What do you know about it?'' All the pent-up emotion of the past months surged forth in Noble like a raging river. ''Lord Almighty, Johnny, I almost died out there! Didn't know who I was for more than two months! Found a woman I loved, had to leave her. Now I'm bound by honor to leave again, all to find Beth! You don't think this thing hasn't caused me grief enough!'' Noble spit out the words.

Johnny stared, his face suddenly hooded. "Then go back to your woman, find her again. Let Beth be."

"I can't do that." Suddenly, Noble almost hated the sister he'd adored since childhood.

"Then give her time." Johnny was already to the front door. "If I see her, what shall I say?"

Noble struggled to his feet, his leg throbbing. "Tell her . . ." He wanted to say she was loved, but couldn't. Beth had made choices he'd never understand. If she had pleaded with Johnny to get her out of the hands of the Kiowa, he would have ridden through hell to do it. If she had said her honor was destroyed and she was too shamed to come home, he would have done the same. But this decision was incomprehensible. The only way he could believe it was to hear it from her own lips.

"Tell her I've promised the colonel I'd bring her home."

The door slammed behind Johnny. It was the end of their years of friendship, the end of Noble's youth. He felt like a very old man as he kneaded the sore muscles of his leg and wondered how he'd tell his father what Johnny had said.

He knew he couldn't. He'd lie, say Johnny had some ideas, that they'd be hunting again with the break in the weather.

He hoped his father didn't know him well enough to see through the prevarication. He feared he did.

Chapter Twenty-three

Johnny hesitated to go to Beth again. He didn't put it past Noble to track him to her. His own tribe had thought him smitten with a woman. He'd told his friend that he sought someone who meant much to him during his sojourn with the Kiowa, and Fast Cloud had laughed knowingly. Since the last raids of autumn, Johnny's prestige had risen like the moon, and he now had horses and status in the warrior's society. It would be logical to find a wife.

The Kiowa still raided toward Texas, but Beth's band stayed nearer to Fort Larned than Johnny thought wise. The Oglala and some Southern Brule had ridden south, leaving the Platte. Johnny sensed the spring bringing more raiding, more provocation to the white eyes. There would be repercussions, and he wanted Beth to be safe. The white eyes brought many troops to Fort Larned in April, and they torched a large village of Cheyenne and Sioux.

But the grass was scarce, and the cavalry horses couldn't survive on so little, so not many People died in the early spring. But summer brought steady raiding.

Johnny heard that Beth's band moved south of the Arkansas.

Johnny rode the back of the summer's path of destruction with his band, trying to warn them that the Army wouldn't tolerate the roads and railroads and coaches being rubbed out. Some heeded his warnings, some thought him still too white. He gave up trying, and the raiding that summer was better than it had been in many years. But the new iron road was cutting the path of the buffalo. It divided tribes as well. The time for destruction of the road was coming, and with it, many whites would die. Johnny sensed he had to move quickly.

He saddled up, feeling the time was right to find her again, explaining to Fast Cloud he'd be back. This time, he knew his friend believed him. Summer had brought them both much glory, many horses.

It was late fall, as Johnny reined in at the edge of Beth's camp. Before greeting the chief with his proper respect, he wanted to see Beth without being seen, to judge her, to weigh her wishes against Noble's determination. She was easy to sight—her blond head, taller than most, bobbed out of a lodge. Her presence garnered respect as everyone greeted her warmly. She was a different person from the Beth he'd known, a young, pretty, and vivacious girl, but somehow discontented. Now the girl was a woman, calm, self-assured, happy with herself. Her blond hair gleamed among the dark hair all around her, and her dress was one of softest skins, beautifully beaded. He was proud of her. More than that, he respected her. Tales of her visions, and their accuracy, had spread quickly among the tribes. She was a woman of place and power.

He wasn't so sure of himself. Watching Beth, he realized that she'd found a fulfillment she would never have attained in the white world. She would never need a man to make her complete.

He nudged his horse into camp. A bevy of children shrieked, and she twisted. Concern wiped from her face as she saw him. Greeting him warmly, her smiling eyes blue in a tanned face, a line of freckles bridging her cheeks, she glowed. He pressed her palm to his, noting the calluses and roughness of hands well used. She didn't ask why he'd come. They were suddenly easy with each other in a way that was new for him.

This time his arrival met with less suspicion and foreboding.

"Greetings, sister."

Beth nodded, her hello shining forth like sunshine. "Come to my tepee, Little Fox. Magpie and Grandfather will be so pleased to see you again."

"And you, Mythmaker?" He had to ask.

"I too welcome you, Little Fox."

He searched for more in her eyes, but found only genuine friendship. It was enough, for now.

The weather had turned dark, clouds threatened snow once again, and he prolonged his stay. He'd had only a few moments alone with Beth. The raiding party against the Navajo had turned out as she'd predicted, with Struck His Head Against a Tree killed. Once more, her prophecy, once told by her grandfather, had enhanced her reputation as a mythmaker.

He knew he had tried his best to tell Noble the truth, and that it made no difference to Noble. Noble's promise to his father came first; it was almost an obsession. Beth had to know. Johnny agonized over how to tell her she would be found, that the Army would come one day in the not too distant future. The new construction at Fort Larned had surprised him until he'd realized they were readying it for more troops. The inevitability of the coming conflict would probably mean she would be found, exchanged, traded for, and eventually, returned to Fort Larned.

With the September raids over, Johnny reached the conclusion that he must speak with Mythmaker. He seized his chance one evening in late autumn. He chanced upon her alone in her tepee, Magpie with his grandfather for a story-telling. Hesitating at the entrance, he tried to rehearse tactful arguments, but nothing came to him. He felt as awkward as a boy with his first girl.

"May I enter?" He ducked his head around the flap, speaking in English this time.

"Of course," Beth answered in English. She smiled, seeing his surprise. "I don't want to forget my English. I will teach all the little ones someday."

"You'll never forget. It's the children, the ones who

are taken captive when young, who forget. They're never able to return to the white world, if they've been accepted into the tribe and raised as one of our own.''

Johnny worked his way beside her, careful not to come between her and the fire in the middle of the tepee. He longed to stroke her face, touch her hair, but this was not the time. There were other things, painful subjects, that had to be spoken of first. The silence pulled between them like rawhide on a rack.

''You want to say something to me, something you'd rather not say?'' Beth spoke hesitantly, as though she didn't want his answer.

''You never knew what I thought, before. You should be worried, but if you can see my thoughts, I won't have to find the words.''

She smiled gently. ''I sensed your uneasiness, that's all. You can say anything to me you wish.''

Johnny settled beside her, watching her hands as they continued to work the leather on her lap. She was braiding a halter, her fingers smoothing the plaits with a sureness that belied her lack of experience.

''You have found life here easier than you expected.'' It was a statement of fact, and he expected no answer.

''No. Just different. Once I found my place here, it became easier than before. I almost died in the first months, as I told you. But now it is my life.''

''Beth . . . '' He didn't know how to continue. ''Beth, you know Noble won't stop searching. I spoke with him. He'll find your bones, or you. I can't stop him. There was no way I could lie.''

She became still, her hands halted in midbraid. Her face was almost gray. ''I thought that was the reason you came back. Maybe I should write him a letter, something to let him know I've chosen to stay here, and he should let me go.''

''It won't be enough. He'll have to hear it from you. He feels he owes it to you, to your father. To himself. You know how stubborn he is.''

Beth looked at her suddenly still hands. ''As pig-headed as you, Johnny. You found me.''

His eyes sought hers as he gently lifted her chin in his fingers. ''I wanted to go home to my tribe, it was time to get back a part of me I'd lost.'' He knew she understood what he was trying to say. ''But Noble will come. And we're blood brothers.''

Her pale eyes held his, fear, hope, love, and understanding flashing into his dark ones. They both knew there was only one solution. ''How can I leave? They need me. . . . ''

''They've rebuilt most of Fort Larned. Stone, this time. More troopers coming. There's going to be war, and soon. All they need is an excuse. You'll be enough. Rescue the colonel's daughter, and all that. Once Noble tracks us down . . . ''

For a moment, fear seized her. She had noticed the ''us.'' ''How will we be able to leave?''

''You can do as you wish. You are Mythmaker. But

Noble will find you, or die trying. I don't matter. Just another Comanche.''

She stroked the halter, sensing its symmetry and purposefulness. ''He makes his own decisions. He is a man.''

She wasn't going to leave with him; he felt the battle was over. He watched her hair hide her face, her turmoil suddenly stilled. He'd never appreciated her true beauty before. It wasn't in the small bones of her face, the large eyes, the kind yet firm mouth. She'd wanted to be needed all her life, and the truth of it struck him like a buffalo hit by a bullet from a Sharps rifle. She belonged to her people. Her tribe.

Noble and the colonel hadn't needed her, although they'd protected and cherished her; their lives had been complete in their male world of action and discipline. Beth had needed that same action and discipline. Her inner strengths, her deep faith, had emerged and blossomed within the tribe, and as shaman she had found action. Her need was answered, her prayers met.

''If there is a way to bring Noble to you, shall I do it?''

Her face clouded again, her eyes narrowing. ''It wouldn't do him—or me—any good. I'm not the Beth he knew.''

''But he deserves the truth. A shaman does not lie.''

''No, but will he believe the truth? Or seek to make his own?''

He was prouder of her in that moment than he'd

ever been of anyone in his entire life. She was truly a woman of the People now.

"It will be up to him."

They sat apart, the fire between them. Its warmth ruddied her cheeks. She was more beautiful to him than any woman, more beautiful than she'd ever been in her white people's clothes, chasing after her brother as a child.

"If there is a way, will you speak with him?" He didn't know yet what would happen, but he'd divert calamity if he could. Beth would never let her presence in the tribe bring disaster upon her people, of that he was sure.

She nodded slowly, her eyes never leaving his. "If it is the only way."

They both knew what they meant. Peace, harmony, protection of her people, of his, was all-important. Self would be sacrificed for the greater good.

"Can you see the future, Shaman?" He spoke now in Kiowa.

Her eyes tightened. "I saw it long ago, my friend."

She never told him what it was to be. He knew better than to ask.

Chapter Twenty-four

It seemed to Noble that it took forever for him to find Rebecca's homestead. When he finally sighted its familiar outline, every bit of him wanted to scream out to her, to say he'd come back to wed her once and for all.

But he couldn't do that. He had to tell her the truth, that his promise still bound him, even more than he'd known before. Night was settling in, its wintery hues darkening the soddy to a black block, matching his mood. He'd lost his best friend and his sister to the same enemy, the Indians. One of them he could still try to bring back.

"Hello, the house!" he shouted through cupped hands.

A lone light flickered through the oiled window as a shadow appeared in the opened doorway, and he knew he'd printed her form in his mind as a part of his eternal memory. Aching to hold her, he roweled his horse into a canter.

"Noble?"

He heard her strong voice carry without ever rising above a normal tone. Silhouetted by the light behind

163

her, she filled the small doorway. Through the thin material of her nightgown, he could see her shapely figure, and ached for her.

"It's me, Rebecca." Reining in, he threw himself to the ground, grabbing her into his arms, searching for her lips. They clung together breathlessly, kissing deeply.

Finally, Rebecca pulled back. "I'd guess the news is good, Noble. Find out what you needed?"

Pulling her into the soddy, he clung to her. "I'm not married, Rebecca. Never have been. The woman in my dream, she's my sister."

"Oh," Rebecca breathed out softly. "So why'd you come back, Noble McFarland?"

He knew what she expected. "Can't promise anything yet, Rebecca. Truth is, I've still got to find her. I think I know where she is, but an old friend of mine says she won't come home, that she actually wants to stay"—he hesitated, steeling himself—"with the Kiowa. I don't believe him." Can't believe him, he wanted to say. It didn't matter either way; he had to hear from Beth herself that she'd become someone he never knew and could never understand. The possibility was too staggering for him.

Rebecca sank her head into his shoulder. "So you're going after her, to the Kiowa?"

"If I have to. Right now, I do."

She was silent, tracing endless whorls with her fingernail on his sleeve.

"Hang up your hat and stay awhile, cowboy." Her smile was sad. "Got a stew on the fire."

"You're always taking care of me, Rebecca. One day, I'll do the taking care. Promise me you'll wait."

Her back to him, Rebecca spooned a wooden bowl with food. "No promises, not now, Noble. May not be able to keep them. We'll see, if and when you come back."

They both knew she didn't expect him to live. Yet there was no way he could fathom her despair at losing another man she'd grown to love, and she'd never show him the truth.

Settling across the plank table from him, she raised her eyes finally to his.

"So eat. You look like a scarecrow." Her smile was wry.

He wanted to explain his despair, his horror at his sister's decision, but knew she already understood.

"I'll be leaving tomorrow. Early. Sooner this gets done, sooner I'll be back." He hardly tasted the food.

"Get your bedroll in then, put your horse up in the shed. Soon as you finish up . . ."

Clasping her hand across the table, he shook his head for silence. "Can I just hold you tonight, Rebecca? Promise, that's all I want."

Dipping her head, she stared at their intertwined fingers. "I wish we could have more."

How could he tell her he couldn't believe Johnny, that Elizabeth had to be held a captive against her will?

It was impossible that his refined, gentle sister would have become an Indian. "We will, soon as I get Elizabeth. Won't be long."

She shoved their half-empty bowls together, and standing, began to untwine her braid. "Sooner you get on the road, sooner you'll come riding over my hill. Be ready for bed, and get your horse settled."

Watching the winter stars, waiting for the cusp of Spring, he patted the Army mount's neck absently. He wanted to love her more than he wanted to find Elizabeth, and the truth galled him. But he would not break his promise to her, nor to his father. First, he'd find Johnny and learn the exact tribe holding Rebecca.

Rebecca's blue nightgown was the color of her eyes, and they shined as he crawled into the bed beside her, leaving only his boots and his jacket beside her bed. Her red hair spreading on his arm, she snuggled close, sighing softly. All night long, he twirled her hair in his finger, and tried to sleep.

He knew she'd not gotten a wink, either.

Chapter Twenty-five

Tepees stretched as far as Beth could see, their decorations dancing on the hides as her eyes ached with trying to count them. They were finally camped, a few miles from the site of the summer's sacred Medicine Lodge. Her hands, with an action separate from her conscious thought, twisted in knots. She'd trusted Johnny this far, and she had to continue with that trust. He'd been right about the summer's raids bringing repercussions.

She helped with the tepee poles, quickly setting stakes, arranging the flaps at the top to let the smoke drift out. The leaders among her people converged in the adjoining camp of the Kiowa-Comanche. Beth worked with the rote motions, working leather thongs through stakes, setting the pins, arranging her gear in its proper position within her lodge. While she tidied and fretted with the flaps, her mind hurried toward the future like a camp dog attracted to the offal pile.

Gowned in her oldest, dowdiest work dress, she set to work. While her fingers built the fire and started a meal, she forced herself to concentrate on her current patients. She'd check on the boy with the burned arm and the woman about to deliver. There was no time to sit around waiting for Johnny and what he had arranged. If Johnny wanted to see her, he'd find her. If Noble was with him, they'd find her as she was. She wasn't about to dawdle about in her best dress, shoving at her fingernails.

Magpie and Grandfather trotted up close to dark. The boy slid from his spotted pony, excitement shimmering about him like moonglow. She sensed Grandfather's reserve.

"Hungry?" She smiled, knowing they had probably dined with others, they were so late.

"We could always eat more of your good food, Daughter." Grandfather swung his leg over the withers, gesturing for the boy to lead them to the herd.

She seethed with questions, her clarity of thought ripping apart. "What news, Grandfather?"

Settling in his place of honor in the tepee, he accepted a small bowl from her. "There are many of us here, Mythmaker. The white agents say the white leaders will be here soon with many gifts. They must have many, if they wish to stop the young men from such a profitable pursuit as stealing from our enemies!" He chuckled.

The past summer had been good to those who stayed north of the Arkansas. Horses and glory returned with them to their tribes. Beth knew the depth of provocation that had brought the Army to bow to the peacemakers.

If this treaty commission didn't work out, it would mean total war.

She scrutinized Grandfather's weathered face. Although he bent to eat her stew, she knew he waited. Quieting herself, she walked around the fire, to his side.

Their camp was wedged between the Kiowa-Comanche and the Prairie Apache. The smaller trees were gold and red, here on the banks of Medicine Lodge Creek. She could see the persimmon loaded on trees as she stared into the groves. It would be too rude to prompt Grandfather.

"I heard that the Arapaho arrived early. Black Kettle, of the Cheyenne, sent his family with them. He wants peace, with the desperation of a fox run to ground. His Dog Soldiers do not follow him."

Beth felt a chill mantle her. Fighting off a sense of death, she searched the clearing in the last light, for signs of Magpie's return.

"When will the whites arrive?"

"Soon. It is said, they bring many wagons and troops from the fort. Why they believe we will take blankets for our land is the thinking of the dim-witted."

Beth knew all too well how they were thinking, that a bright bit of wool and some beads, flour, sugar, and empty promises would be more than enough. They wanted the land, the earth the Indians knew was no one's to sell or barter. And the white eyes would take it, one way or another.

"Will the Cheyenne come too?"

Grandfather snorted. "Ha. Those. They'll squat on their haunches, see what kind of a day we have. Maybe they'll wander in to take their bribes. But we'll do the work while they wait."

"Isn't it time for their Medicine Arrow ceremonies?"

Grandfather nodded. "They'll make it time. Black Kettle will have to risk all to stay here, if they make their medicine. I wonder if he dares?"

She couldn't wait any longer. "Any signs of Little Fox?"

His mouth full, Grandfather shook his head. "I think he must have gone to the fort to do what he must. He'll come with the Army, Granddaughter. Perhaps he can tell us the truth of what they are thinking, these men who say they want peace."

She knew he was right. But every inch of her ached to have the interview over, to get the final scene played and the curtain down. Then she'd be truly free.

"They want peace, but their kind . . . "

Grandfather put down his empty gourd. "Is there something we should know, Shaman? A vision?"

The cold chill of death wouldn't leave her. "Nothing specific, my chief. But we'll know death, and soon. There will be no new life from this meeting, here in this sacred place."

His face sagged. "I have felt the same. But Satanta

will speak well for us. He will drive a hard bargain. We must see how it goes.''

Dimly aware of Magpie's entrance, she nodded. Her eyes were too misty to see him clearly. She knew Grandfather would be one of the first to go to live with his ancestors in the next world. But she would never tell him. Nodding to the boy, she wiped her eyes quickly. His excitement barred him from seeing her distress.

''There are so many of us, Grandfather! We are more than any whites!''

She had to tell Magpie the truth. ''That can never be, my child. The whites are more than all the buffalo on the plains, and we will never see the end of them.''

They both stared at her, their faces suddenly clear before her, misery marking them both. They knew she spoke the truth.

''We will see, though.''

The false brightness in her voice echoed like the brass horn blown before a cavalry charge.

Chapter Twenty-six

Johnny felt Noble's reluctance growing with each mile toward the sacred sun-dance grounds. Noble had given his word, he'd speak with Beth alone, before letting his father know she was there. It had taken almost the last shred of their friendship to seal the bargain. But Johnny knew Noble would keep his word, even though it might kill him.

More than 600 whites, including 150 soldiers of the 7th Cavalry and Battery B of the 4th Artillery, complete with Gatling guns, trampled the prairie grass a few miles from the lodges of the tribes. Johnny slipped in among the entourage of correspondents, translators, and camp followers like the son of the Commissioner of Indian Affairs. He and Noble dressed as scouts, trying to blend in. Neither of them spoke much beyond what was absolutely necessary. Framing advice in his mind, Johnny found the words lumped in his throat. Noble didn't want to hear any of it. Beth alone could make him believe.

Johnny slipped away as General Harney, warned of a Dog Soldier attack, circled the ambulances a half mile from the council grounds. The wagons rimmed the camp, a precaution against the Cheyenne who still longed to avenge their burned village.

The Kiowa numbered almost 150 lodges. Boldly riding the edge of the camp, Johnny searched for Beth's distinctive tepee design. Dogs yipped at his horse's heels as dusk fell quickly on the October night. He almost hoped he wouldn't find her.

But he did. "Shaman, may I enter?"

He heard her voice from within, small but firm. "Of course, brother of my brother. I have been waiting."

The boy and Grandfather nodded politely, giving him a sad yet polite greeting.

"Is anyone with you, cousin?" The old chief raked Johnny's face with eyes still fiercely protective.

"No, not now. I am alone."

He could feel tension leaking from the lodge like smoke through the flaps. "May I speak with Myth-maker, Grandfather? Alone?"

It was rude, but he had to try once more to convince Beth she had to go back, back to Noble and the life she no longer wanted.

Magpie and Grandfather slipped silently out the door flap.

"He is here. Your father also. I've told Noble you'll speak with him as soon as possible."

Beth almost laughed. "How like him. So impatient. Everything has to be done yesterday. He would have made a good soldier."

"When shall I bring him?"

She'd already decided. "Tomorrow. The peace commissioners meet in the morning with our chiefs, so afterward. I will wait here."

"And then?" He already knew her answer.

"Then I will live my life, and he can tell my father the truth. The truth does set free, Johnny, just as the white religion preaches. How is he?"

"Silent. He feels betrayed. As though he has sacrificed everything to find you, lost the only love he's truly wanted for the rest of his days, all because of you. And you don't want his sacrifice."

"Then that is his choice. If he chooses to spill his blood for me, then so be it. I can make no other path but my own."

He wanted to reach out for her, to stroke her hand in his. "You are more Indian in your thoughts every minute."

"Not so much Kiowa, as my own. My freedom to think as I choose." She saw the longing in his eyes.

"And what do you say, Johnny Two Hats? Do you still walk in two directions, or have you made your choice?"

"I cannot go back. My choice was made three seasons ago when I chose to raid with my people." He leaned across the dim space between them, the soft glow of the fire burnishing her tanned face to copper. Her hand was a small fist in his as he gently uncurled the tense talons of her fingers. Tracing the lines of her palm with his forefinger, he was swept into her sorrow at the hurt she knew she must bring to her brother, to her father. He would have done anything to take it from her.

"Tomorrow, then. After the council meets."

He nodded. "Be careful, Mythmaker. There are many whites out there, searching for captive women and children. If you are seen, you could be forced to go back by the commissioner. There are also those men along who scribble on paper all the time, drink, and laugh loudly. They send stories to the big newspapers. You would become a story to be told. Do not let them see you."

Her head no longer bowed over their hands, she arched her neck proudly. "I will not hide among my own people."

She saw the worry in his eyes. "But I thank you. What will happen will be over soon, and then we can go on. All of us."

He hoped she meant to include him too. He would seek her out, after it was over and they were all once again free. As free as the white eyes would let them be.

Chapter Twenty-seven

The council lodge, a twenty-foot arbor of elm and cottonwood, arched on the north bank of the Medicine Lodge Creek. The cool winds of autumn carried a hint of rain to come. The commissioners perched on camp stools, elbows poking into folding tables, as the generals, the governor of Kansas, the lieutenant governor, the senators, Commissioner of Indian Affairs Taylor, a motley crew of cynical newspapermen, and soldiers stared at the ring of logs covered with tribal chiefs decked out in the finest duds. The pipe was passed, and for all except the Comanche, who were in camp but not at the sacred site, and the Cheyenne, who still lurked on the Cimarron forty miles away, the Peace Commission commenced.

It was a quick beginning. Twenty suits of clothes went to each tribe, a foretaste of all the wonderful things to come from treading the white man's road. Beth knew Satanta, Satank, and the other leaders of the Kiowa weren't fooled. They would hear the terms of peace and decide if it was worth it. However they chose, Beth knew there was no turning back now—for any of them.

She left word with Magpie where she could be found. A woman about to deliver needed her. Hugging the boy, she warned him not to worry, she would return. She touched him, probing his thin shoulders with her fingers.

"I am with you always, my child. Do not forget."

Taking her supplies, the soft leathers and herbs, she wound her way through the camp as early evening settled in. Bits of talk assailed her, try as she might to ignore them. Everyone spoke of what would happen when the commission started in earnest, when the white man named Henderson spoke words from the Great Father in Washington that would bring peace, or war. She was always cold, no matter how many blankets she wrapped about her.

The horses behind her stopped. In an instant, she knew who would speak her name. Her old name.

"Beth. My God, Beth?"

He had aged in the time she'd been gone. The gangly boy was gone, and the beard-shadowed face staring at her was so close to that of their father's, she'd have sworn time had reversed.

"Yes, Noble." She held her ground. He would have to come to her first.

In a flurry, Noble stumbled from the horse, almost falling. Racing to him, she dropped her bundle, her blankets, and wrapped him in her strong arms.

"Noble, it's me," she whispered through tears. "You've grown so, I thought you were the colonel, a young man." Stroking his hair, his hat in her hand, she wanted to see him more clearly in the fading light. He shut his eyes and pulled her closer. She could feel his suffering, all his anguish pouring into her.

"Come back with me, tonight. This instant. You can take Johnny's horse. . . . " he choked into her ear.

Untangling herself from him, she stooped to redrape her blanket over her shoulders. Her blond braids lay brightly against the dark wool. It was a fine Navajo blanket, a true prize. But she knew he saw only a squaw woman clad in dirty leather and a scrap of wool.

"No, Noble. Not tonight. Not now. Not ever."

He stumbled back from her, catching his heel in her medicine bundle. "Good Lord Almighty, you can't mean it! You really mean to stay here, with these savages?"

She'd never heard him use that word before. It was as though all the prejudice of his race was spilling forth for the first time, a spew of ugliness she knew wasn't truly how he thought. At least, it wasn't how he'd thought when they were children.

Johnny had retreated, giving them what privacy he could. She knew she could never take him to her lodge and introduce him to Magpie and Grandfather. He'd never understand how much she cared for them. It would have to end here, tonight, under the night sky.

"Yes, I do. Johnny told you the truth. Nothing you say will change my mind."

"What about the fact they're a dead people already?

You know what they're planning, don't you? All those fancy men in their city suits? They're gonna stick the tribes on reservations, turn 'em into regular farmers. And if they don't go willingly, they're gonna die. Simple as that, Beth. And you'll die with them. Can't you see, you have to come home?''

She waited for his next attempt at persuasion in silence. Let him spill it out, like a spring creek becoming a small flood.

"You belong with us. At the fort. Or somewhere else, if you like. The colonel will send you back East, if you want. Do anything you ask. You know it, I know it. Just ask. Please.''

It was almost more than she could stand. She was pummelled by his pleas, assaulted by his passion.

"I will not, Noble.'' There was no sense in pleading for his understanding. "Tell Father what I have told you. If he needs to hear it from me, so be it.''

Head bent, he stared at her feet. "Is it really as Johnny said? You're a shaman? A healer?''

"Yes.'' She knew it was impossible for him to believe. "I was on my way to deliver a baby, just now.''

"Oh.''

"Can I see you again—and Father, if he wishes? As long as we are here?'' It sounded lame, she knew. But the fight had gone from Noble like blood from a severed artery. She wanted, above all, to be kind. She still loved them, but from a distance.

"I'll let Johnny know. He'll bring Father, if he wants to talk to you himself."

Her arms ached to hold him, but she knew it was useless. "That would be good." Snatching up her supplies, she peered into the deepening shadows for a glimpse of Johnny's face.

Johnny was stony in his silence. It struck her, with the force of a tornado, that he was an Indian now. There would be no more pull between the two parts of him.

Noble jerked into the saddle, yanking on the reins.

"Noble, be happy. Be free of me. Go your own way." She wanted to add, "if you can."

Noble followed Johnny from the camp. Beth stared at her brother's back until her eyes ached and darkness swallowed him.

Chapter Twenty-eight

The first day of serious treaty discussion didn't go all that well. White Bear eloquently summed up the sentiments of the assorted tribes when he said, ''When the buffalo leave the country, we will let him the Great Father know. By that time we will be ready to live in houses.''

Beth stayed close to her camp, her band not so hospitable to the roving correspondents who swarmed to the Arapaho, invited to their lodges by an overanxious Little Raven. Johnny had dropped Noble at the circle of wagons, Noble never looking back as he showed his pass and slipped into the encircled canvas tents.

Grandfather returned the second day, October 21, 1867, by the white man's calendar, with the results.

''They have won. We are to be caged on lands like men in their prisons. They agreed to let us hunt on our own lands south of the Arkansas, so long as there are buffalo. As long as there are buffalo!'' His voice shook.

Remembering the piles of bones scattering the prairies, Beth sank at his feet. ''Sit, Grandfather, sit,'' she urged.

Only a few days earlier they had heard of the slaugh-

ter of a big herd by the soldiers and the men who rode
with the peace commission to Medicine Lodge Creek.
Only Satanta had been able to stop it, his anger echoed
by General Harney, who ordered some of the hunters
arrested. Hundreds of buffalo had been left to rot. The
white man would make sure there were no more buffalo.

"We are to be given houses, medicine houses, doc-
tors, blacksmiths, teachers for the children. What can
they teach us? We are to be made white, Shaman. As
though we would want to be!"

The end was not so far down the road, the white
man's road. The Kiowa as she knew them would be
gone before the end of her life. Leaving Grandfather
in their lodge, Beth ducked into the evening air. Huge,
dark clouds thundered across the sky, rolling with the
wind. It carried away their spirits, the past of the
Kiowa. She sensed their future slipping away, and it
was like grasping the wind to halt it. Clutching her
arms tightly to her, she prayed for the strength to know
what was right. Rain spattered her face, soaked her
hair, and worked in fast-running rivulets down her
back. It was as though the heavens wept for the People.

One woman alone could not change the course of
history. Her powerlessness overwhelmed her, tears
melting with the rain. But she could be the teacher
they needed. Perhaps she could ease the way onto the
white man's road for the children. It was too late for

most of them, but they needed her now, more than they ever had.

Silently, she said farewell one last time to her father, seeing him in her mind propped on a camp chair in his tent, his uniform opened at the neck as he read one of his treasured books. She hadn't truly said her good-byes to him until that moment.

"Grandfather, where is Magpie? We must sleep now, for tomorrow we must go home."

There was a hint of of a smile in his eyes. "Home? To that piece of earth no bigger than my thumbnail they call a reservation? Home, when we have lost our lands for as far as we could ride?"

She wasn't about to let him slide away from her. Despair killed more swiftly than the white man's diseases. "Yes, home. We have work to do."

The next morning winter nipped at their hands as they worked to strike their camp. An old chief, a child, a young woman of the Kiowa, and one Comanche brave slipped away from the Medicine Lodge Treaty grounds as a dark dawn worked its way into day.

Chapter Twenty-nine

The return to Fort Larned had been interminable for Noble. Each day he felt his lie to his father growing upon his soul like a carbuncle. It was the only way. Beth had forced the untruth upon him, forced him to find his freedom in deceit.

The colonel had shrunk into his uniform as Noble relayed his lie. "Dead, sir. For sure. I spoke with the man who took her. It wasn't long after her capture."

The colonel hadn't asked for details. "Did Johnny find her before she died?"

"No. After he heard, he came for me. Took us this long to track down the exact band." The falsities rolled off his tongue more easily now.

"Thank him for me. Tell him he can come back to duty now."

"Don't think he's planning on it, sir." The unspoken fire hung between them.

"You too, son? Leaving me?"

For the first time, Noble sat before his father without asking permission. "Have to. Rebecca's waiting. At least, I hope she is."

"The woman who took care of your leg?"

Noble nodded. "I'll write. Let you know."

His father seemed to shrink further. "Losing you too."

"You never needed me, Father. Not like you needed her."

Anger flashed in the colonel's eyes. "You never needed me, son. Long ago, you decided where you were heading. Just luck you stayed scouting so long, only way to keep you around until you were full grown. Sometimes, I thought you'd light out on your own when you were just a tadpole." A twinge of a smile accompanied the memory of Noble as a boy.

Noble knew he was right. "You raised us both that way, Father. Do what we thought right. Go our own way, to hades with what the rest of 'em thought. Best way to raise a kid I can think of. I'll do the same with my own."

The colonel stretched forth his hand, palm open. "Come visit me, son, and bring those grandchildren with you."

"You too, colonel. Come any time."

Noble stood for hours in the cold dark of night, staring at his father's silhouette on the walls of the canvas tent. Long before dawn, he saddled up, his own pony this time, not a cavalry mount.

He could see Rebecca's red hair shining in the morning sun before him. Even though it was promising to be a gray, wet day, the trail back to her was warm and sunny in his heart.